FALLING FOR A HOOD KING 2

SHVONNE LATRICE

ABOUT THE AUTHOR

Other Works by Me:

Good Girls Love Thugs 1-5
Falling for a Hood King 1-4
Married to a Distinguished Thug 1-3
She's Gotta Have It 1-2
Me & My Dope Boy 1-3
Yazir & Nina 1-3
Forbidden Love with a Thug 1-3
You Needed Me 1-3
Shorty is in Love with a Real One 1-4
I Got Your Back 1-2
My Baby Is a West Coast King 1-4
Our Love Is the Realest 1-3
She Got It Bad for a Heartless Gangsta 1-4
She Got It Bad for a Heartless Gangsta: An AK Christmas
Hood Boyz Fall In Love Too 1-3
Nobody Can Love You Like Them Roughnecks Do 1-4
She Gave Her All to the Hood's Finest 1-5

Visit www.theshvonnelatrice.com for paperbacks!

facebook.com/ShvonneLatrice
twitter.com/siobhannoir
instagram.com/siobhannoir

$14.99

ISBN 978-1-966375-00-5

"**W**ake yo' ass up!"

I opened my eyes and realized I was staring down the barrel of a gun. I jumped back and saw it was Greg holding it.

"Greg, what the fuck are you doing?" I asked, as I tried to crawl up the headboard. I was scared as hell.

"I'm just doing my job. Now get the fuck up and let's go," he ordered and waved the gun.

"Go where?" I asked.

"Stop asking questions and get the fuck up!" he boomed.

I jumped up and slid on my flip-flops. Thank God I laid down in my skinny jeans and t-shirt, because I usually sleep in my underwear and bra.

"Can I just get my baby Greg, let me just take my son with us," I pleaded.

"Hurry the fuck up!" he yelled making me jump.

I rushed to the other bedroom and picked up my baby. I grabbed his diaper bag and car seat, and then came out of the room. Greg was pacing the living room as if he was thinking, with his gun still in his hand. I tried to think of a way to escape or call for help, but I knew nothing would work at this point.

"You got everything you need for that little nigga?" he asked once he noticed me emerge from the back.

"Yeah, I do," I replied, nodding.

"Come on," he said, waving his gun towards the door. As we walked out, he kept his gun pressed into my back. "Don't do nothing stupid, bitch." he said through gritted teeth, as we neared his truck.

He kept the gun pressed to my back, as I buckled Jackson into the car seat as slowly as I could.

"Can I get back here with him?"

"No, get yo' pretty ass in the front seat with me," he smirked and then smacked my ass.

I closed the back door, and then hopped in on the passenger side. He ran around quickly, and climbed in the driver's seat. I wanted to pull out my phone and call Julius or anybody, but I knew his ass would shoot me. He's hated me ever since our first encounter at CVS that night.

A tear slid down my cheek as Greg pulled off from the curb. He kept one hand on the wheel and one hand on his gun trigger. I had no idea what his plans were and that made it even scarier.

I sat in the warehouse, staring at a passed out Natalia. She was beautiful as hell, but I hated her personality. She always tried to play that innocent role, when she knew she was probably out here busting it open for any and everybody. I wanted to fuck her so badly, but that wasn't part of the plan. I easily could though, because she was unconscious in this chair I tied her to. I thought as I rubbed my chin hair. I'd made her put her baby to sleep as soon as we arrived, and then I knocked her ass out with one good hit in the head. I laughed to myself as I recalled the events.

Hey, don't look at me like the bad guy; I'm just doing my damn job. I need to make money and eat just like y'all muthafuckas. And as you know, Julius didn't even put me on when he moved out to Charleston. I low-key hated that nigga, but it wasn't enough to come after his people. Someone else hated him that much, and that's where I came in. So as a wise person once said, don't kill the messenger.

See, my boss, Hugo asked me to kidnap old sexy ass Natalia. The job paid $8,000, and I needed it bad. It was chump change to what Julius and them niggas was making down in South Carolina, but shit, it was something. Anyway, Hugo's nephew has a thing for Natalia, so he concocted all this shit in order to be her knight in shining armor.

Once he saved Natalia, she would fall in love with him and leave Julius. He planned to skip off up to Michigan, until Julius cooled off. I warned him that Julius would never cool off about this, but nobody listens to my ass.

I laughed at my thoughts, 'cause this nigga Hugo's nephew was definitely coo coo for coco puffs. He's read too many damn fairytales in his life if he thought this shit was gonna work. It seemed no matter what anyone said, or how fucked up Julius treated this little hoe, she never strayed. Plus, it's too much pussy in Indianapolis alone to be drumming up plans and schemes for it.

I looked at my watch because Natalia started to stir. I text the nigga to see what he was up to, and he let me know he would be pulling up in about ten minutes. I nodded as if he could see me, and then smiled big as I saw Natalia coming to.

"Greg, why are you doing this?" she slurred with her eyes squinted.

She had a knot on her head from when I knocked her ass out. I shook my head and lit a cigarette. Even though she was messed up, she was still fine as hell. I needed this cigarette to stop me from testing that pussy out. I knew it had to be good, if she was able to have Julius out here acting psycho for her. I knew it couldn't have been the conversation.

"Shut the fuck up!" I yelled after taking a pull. I couldn't think of a lie to tell her, so being an asshole was the next best thing.

I got the text that Hugo's nephew was here, and it was time to put on a show. I counted down in my head, and then the weak ass warehouse door, came flying down. Both Natalia and I turned our heads to see what it was, although I already knew.

"Frank! Oh my gosh! Please help me!" Natalia yelled to him, as she squirmed in the chair.

"I got you ma." he said rushing towards her.

"Aye nigga, the fuck you doing?" I asked putting on my act.

"Taking my girl! Don't get fucked up!" he yelled and I almost laughed at his soft ass. Little nigga couldn't even get pussy on his own, and he got the nerve to be acting all hard.

"Where is my gun?" I asked, continuing on with my scripted words.

"Shut the fuck up!" Frank yelled, pulling a gun from his waist.

He kept it pointed at me, as he, Natalia, and her baby backed out of the warehouse. Once, they were out of sight, I lit a blunt and chilled out for a bit. I prayed for his sake that Julius didn't find him, because he'd be long fucking gone if he did.

JULIUS TATE

Natalia missed her flight two days ago. I called her nonstop and constantly text her phone with no response. I immediately flew back to Indianapolis, to find the door to my house wide open. My heart almost stopped, as I came to the realization that someone had kidnapped my baby girl and son. The worst part was the fact that I had no idea who would do this. I immediately thought Hugo, but I had no damn proof. I was gonna go crazy if I didn't find them soon. My heart literally ached at the thought of someone harming either one of them.

I was lying in my bed, thinking about my baby girl. I had a glass of Hennessey in one hand, a picture of her in a bikini when we were in Los Angeles in the other hand, and a gun on my lap. Tears escaped my eyes, as I silently stared at the TV not even paying attention to what was on it. I hadn't cried since my mother passed, but I couldn't help it. Suddenly, my phone rang, snapping me out of my thoughts. Without looking, I went ahead and answered it.

"Hello?" I sniffled.

"Julius, baby, are you okay?" Bianca asked in a concerned tone.

I was quiet for a moment, as I gathered my thoughts together. "Actually nah, I'm not. Someone kidnapped my girl and my kid; my fucking kid that's only been here two damn weeks. I knew I shouldn't have left them." I shook my head. Bianca was silent for a moment, which caught my attention. "What do you know?" I asked.

"Well, Julius, I"

"What the fuck do you know!" I yelled standing up. I would kill this bitch in a hot fucking minute if she didn't get to talking.

"Greg! Greg told me he took Natalia and"

I disconnected the call and grabbed my keys. I ran out to my car, and the super cool breeze of the night air didn't bother me like it usually did. I was so angry, that nothing could faze me at this moment. I sped to Greg's apartment complex and hopped out right a-fucking-way. I banged on his door hard as hell, with the butt of my gun. I kicked on the door hard as fuck, when he didn't answer quickly enough.

"Julius, what the fu" He answered the door, and I immediately pressed a gun between his eyes.

"Where is my girl?" I asked through gritted teeth, as I backed him into his apartment. I kicked the door closed with my foot so no nosey neighbors could see.

"Look man, I was just doing my job," he pleaded.

"Where is she Greg? I'm not gone ask again," I said breathing heavily.

"That nigga Frank got her. He took her ass to fucking Troy, Michigan," he spat.

"Nigga, do you really have the nerve to have a fucking attitude with me when you helped this fuck nigga take my bitch?" I frowned in confusion, still holding the gun.

"Hell yeah! What kind of niggas are y'all? Acting all psycho over one little measly bitch! All these hoes out here, and y'all worried about some young ass Natalia!" he yelled.

"You mad 'cause you never fucked?" I chuckled with the gun still pressed between his eyes.

"Actually, when I kidnapped her, I sucked on her clit and"
POW!

I wasn't about to let this nigga disrespect my woman. My clean-up crew was over in South Carolina, so I had to figure some shit out. I knew I couldn't use Hugo's people, 'cause they probably didn't fuck with me anymore, just like their boss. Plus, they were probably in on this kidnapping shit anyway.

I ran to the car for some gloves, duct tape, and alcohol wipes. I ran back up and wiped everything down. I shot Greg in the face a couple more times, until he was unrecognizable, then knocked out every one of his teeth. I chopped his fingertips off, and collected it all. I wrapped his body up in some black trash bags that he had in the house, and taped it tight. I took him to my car, and then drove him to a lake to dump him. I took the brick I found in an alley and taped it around his ankle, before dropping him in. I watched him sink to the bottom as I breathed heavily. That was a lot of fucking work, but it was worth it.

I was tired as hell, but went home to book a flight to Michigan. Frank had crossed his boundaries for the last fucking time, and I had let him live one day too long.

NATALIA

I was so happy that Frank rescued me from crazy ass Greg. That was until I tried to have him take me to the airport and he refused. I pulled my phone out, which was thankfully in Jackson's diaper bag, to call Julius, and he tossed my phone out the window.

"Thank you Frank. Oh my gosh," I panted once he pulled away from the curb.

"Of course ma, I wasn't gone stop until I found you," he smiled.

"Well I appreciate that," I said, leaning over to kiss his cheek. "Can you get me to the Courtyard Hotel?" I asked picking up Jackson's diaper bag.

"For what?" he frowned.

"My flight leaves tomorrow, and that hotel is right by IND airport."

"Nah, we headed somewhere else."

"Frank! No, I have a flight to South Carolina that I need to catch!" I frowned in confusion.

"I don't give a fuck what you had to catch! The plans have changed! Stop trying to run back to that nigga of yours! I'm the one who saved you!" he yelled swerving in and out of his lane.

I pulled out my phone and began to dial Julius, but Frank snatched it from me.

"Frank, give me my phone," I whined as he pulled onto the freeway.

He looked at it, and saw I had Julius cued up on the call screen. He locked it then sat it in his lap.

"What you calling him for? What the fuck you calling him for, when I'm right fuckin' here!" he yelled so loud, that I looked in the backseat to see if he had woken Jackson.

"Frank, just"

"I'm telling you right now Natalia, get over that nigga. I'm tired of chasing yo' stubborn ass. If you can't realize that we belong together on your own, then I will just have to force you," he said as he tossed my iPhone out the window.

"No!" I yelled as I watched my phone crack into pieces, and get ran over by the passing cars.

"Now sit tight until we get to our new home," he said placing his gun in his lap for me to see.

I slid down in my seat and let the tears fall down my face. I had to find a way out of this, for my baby and me.

We had finally arrived to Troy, and checked into a hotel room. Frank was really nervous and hoping Julius didn't find him; I was hoping for the opposite.

"Maybe you should let me call him for you?" I offered.

"What the fuck would that do bitch?" he yelled.

"Let him know I'm okay, so he won't come looking for you," I replied.

"He don't even know I have you, so stop trying to make up reasons to call that nigga!" he scowled at me.

"Frank, ple"

WHAM!

He knocked me upside the head with the butt of the gun. I tried to speak again, but everything faded to black.

I woke up to the sound of my baby crying his eyes out. My head was pounding, and I felt blood on my forehead. I finally gained enough strength to sit up and open my eyes, after lying there for a couple minutes. I realized I was still in the hotel that Frank brought me to, so this was not some nightmare that I prayed for it to be. I looked over and saw Jackson in his carrier, crying as if he was beyond miserable. Although in pain, I needed to tend to my baby. I couldn't let him suffer just because I was.

"It's okay baby," I said as I picked him up.

I walked over to my baby bag to pull out some diapers, a onesie, and some baby bath wash. I bathed Jackson, put on a fresh diaper, and then breast-fed him until he fell asleep. I laid out his little blanket on the bed, and then lay him face down on it. Tears escaped my eyes, as I silently prayed to get out. Suddenly it hit me that Frank wasn't in the room with me. I immediately grabbed the phone and dialed Julius.

"Come on baby, please pick up," I said to myself, as I bounced my leg nervously.

"Hello?"

"Julius! It's me babe." I cried. Hearing his voice immediately brought on the waterworks.

"Natalia, I'm in Troy baby girl, where are you?"

"I'm at a hotel.. I uh.." I stammered as I searched for something with the name of the hotel on it. I finally found a little postcard with Embassy Suites on it. Frank walked into the door just as I was about to speak. "Embassy Suites," I said to Julius calmly.

"Who the fuck is that?" Frank stormed over to me.

"Yes, do you deliver there?" I asked as if I was ordering take out.

"What?" Julius asked confused. I hoped he soon caught on.

"Yes, Embassy Suites on Tower Drive is where I'm at," I repeated. *Come on baby you're a smart guy; catch on*, I said to myself.

"On my way," Julius said, just as Frank snatched the phone.

"Who the fuck was that? I got food," he frowned.

"Well, you've been being so mean to me that I didn't think you had gotten me anything," I replied.

"Well, I did," he spat and shook his head. "Don't make any more calls unless I say it's okay."

"Okay," I nodded. I hoped that Julius was already on his way over here. I wasn't sure how he knew I was in Troy, but I was happy he did.

I got up and headed to the shower. I slowly undressed in the bathroom, as I inspected my head injury. I put my hair up in a tight bun, and then slid in. I let the hot water soothe my sore muscles, as I thought about how far away Julius was from saving me. Right when I turned around to put soap on the towel, I saw Frank in the shower with me. I jumped back and he flashed an evil smile. *I knew I should've locked the door,* I thought.

"F-Frank. What are you doing?" I asked backing up a bit.

"You told me after you had the baby, we would make love. So it's time to pay up," he said walking up and kissing my neck.

"Frank, I don't want to do this," I replied tensing up in his embrace.

"I'm tired of you playing with my fucking emotions Natalia. You're gonna give me what I want! When you had no fucking where to go, who helped you? Me! I was good to you, and yet you telling me you can't give me no pussy because you love a nigga who don't even love you?" he frowned.

"Frank, I"

"Just once, Natalia, just once," he said staring into my eyes. *Don't you open your legs for no other niggas,* Julius' words replayed in my mind.

Only thing you could hear in this moment was the sound of the shower water hitting my body. I stared at him wondering how I could get out of this. I was seventeen years old, I didn't know what the hell to do in this type of situation.

"Ca-can we do it on the bed please?"

"Why?" he frowned.

"It's our first time," I replied nervously.

"Let's go right now," he responded sternly.

I walked past him to step out the shower, and he smacked my ass. I froze up because it stung a little, and because I hated his touch. I dried my feet on the towel I laid on the floor prior to showering, and then grabbed another towel to wrap around myself. I looked over my shoulder as I walked out the bathroom, and saw Frank was not right behind me. I heard him rustling in the bathroom, and I knew now was my chance. I quietly grabbed Jackson, and power-walked to the door. I grabbed the handle, and pulled the door open.

"Where the fuck you going!" I heard Frank yell behind me.

I knew at this moment, it was now or never. I gripped Jackson tightly, and sprinted down the hallway. I quickly glanced back and didn't see Frank. I guess he wanted to get dressed first. All I had on was my towel, and that was all I needed in this moment. I pressed the down button about one hundred times, before the elevator finally came.

"Natalia!" I heard Frank yell.

I quickly slipped on the elevator, and pressed the door close button repeatedly, as if my life depended on it. It finally dinged, letting me know it was gonna close.

"Natalia! You bitch!" I heard Frank's voice coming closer, as the doors closed.

What the fuck am I gonna do? I thought, as Jackson and I rode the elevator down. I had no money, and no phone to see where Julius was. The doors opened, and I walked off quickly. I wanted to run, but I knew I would slip on the marble floors.

"Ma'am, are you okay?" the hotel clerk asked, as I walked by the desk.

I paused and decided to ask her for help. "Yes could you please let me-"

"Natalia!" Frank yelled as he jogged towards me.

I turned away and started running away from him. I looked over my shoulder, to see how close he was, and ran dead smack into something hard.

"I'm sorry, I" I looked up and saw Julius. I had never been so happy to see him in my life. He had on a red t-shirt, black basketball shorts, and the Jordan Retro 1s. His cologne alone, made me feel safe.

He stared past me, glaring at Frank. I looked behind me, and saw Frank slow down until he finally stopped. He panted angrily, and then stood there for a while. Julius took Jackson from me, and then escorted me out the hotel.

"Ma'am! Ma'am, are you alright?" the hotel clerk yelled after me.

I ignored her, as Julius and I walked out. Julius unlocked his rental, and buckled Jackson in some random car seat, as I slid into the passenger side. We drove to his hotel in Birmingham, Michigan and he didn't say a word the whole time.

"I'm sorry Julius," I started.

"Why are you sorry?" he asked as he lay Jackson face down on one of the twin beds.

I shrugged my shoulders, and he picked me up. He dipped his tongue in my mouth, as I wrapped my legs around his waist. He laid me down and then removed my towel. He climbed into bed with me, kicking off his shoes.

"I missed you so much baby girl. Did he touch you?" he asked looking at the gash by my hairline.

"Just that," I replied referring to what he was looking at.

"Why are you only wearing a towel?' he questioned.

"I was trying to shower and he barged in," was all I said.

"And he didn't…" He raised a brow.

"No, he tried, but as you can see I got away," I smiled.

He kissed the palm of my hands and closed his eyes. He pulled me close and hugged me tight as hell. My small frame melted into his strong embrace, and I let out a sigh of relief.

Having Natalia back in my presence gave me an indescribable feeling. I was so damn miserable without her, thinking about how she could possibly be dead or some shit. To make matters worse, my son was with her. I would've lost my whole damn family because of this nigga Frank.

I sat there thinking, as I listened to the shower run. I couldn't let this nigga live through the night; I had to kill him. For him to think he could do some shit like this and go on with his life was unacceptable. Soon as Natalia and Jackson drifted off to sleep, I was heading out to handle Frank's ass.

My thoughts were interrupted, when Natalia came out from the bathroom. She was wrapped in a towel, and her long brown curly hair was sticking to her back. She was squinting, staring at the back of one of the hotel lotions.

"You think this is okay to use?" she frowned.

"Yeah, I'm sure you will be fine. Come here," I chuckled.

She walked over to me and sat in my lap. I stared up into her eyes for a couple moments, and she smiled. I pushed her wet hair behind her ears, and kissed her soft lips.

"I love you. You know that?" I asked.

"I love you too," she replied.

"I'm gonna start being a better man to you," I continued.

"You already are"

"Nah, I'm really not. That whole video you saw wasn't cool. And it wasn't the only time I was fucking around on you," I vented.

She looked away from me and dropped her head. I lifted her chin and turned her face towards me. I kissed her lips and she tensed up.

"Baby, I know I've done a lot. But I'm asking you to forgive me for all that bullshit. I'm gone be dedicated to what we have here. I'm gonna care as much as you do, because I love you. Sound like a plan?" I smiled and she nodded. "You still love the kid?" I smiled.

"You know I do." She cupped my face and stared me in the eyes.

I rolled her over on her back and then opened her towel. I noticed her stomach was already flat, which low key amazed me. I removed my shirt, and then my shorts and boxers. I lay between her soft caramel legs, as she wrapped her arms around my neck and shoulders.

"Fuck, I missed you," I moaned. I was thanking God for sending Natalia to me. I loved her more than anything, and I was blessed that she stuck around through all my bullshit.

"I missed you tooo. Ahhh," she cooed as I entered her tight walls.

I cupped one of her small perky breasts, and sucked on her hard nipples. After paying equal attention to both, I sucked on her lips, as I wound my hips into her pussy. Natalia had the best pussy known to man.

After fucking my wife to sleep, and playing with my son, I crept out of bed. I quietly got dressed, and grabbed my gun. I had a couple homies around Michigan, and it was the only way I could get a gun, since I couldn't bring my own on the plane.

"Where you going?" I heard Natalia whisper.

"Just to handle something," I replied and she got quiet.

I finished tying my shoes and walked over to her. "I'm not going to see any bitches babe, I meant what I was talking about earlier, aight?" she didn't say anything in response. "Aight?" I asked again tickling her.

"Okay, okay!" she laughed and flashed her beautiful smile.

"You're so beautiful Natalia," I said more so to myself than her.

She smiled and stared up into my eyes. I leaned down to kiss her lips, and she held onto my face as I did.

After assuring my baby girl, I headed towards the door. I stopped in my tracks and remembered I needed more information from Natalia. I was gonna ask her for Frank's room number, cause I had no idea what room he was in.

"Babe, what room were you staying in at Embassy?" I asked.

"212," she replied groggily. "Why?" she inquired.

"Just wondering," I replied nonchalantly. I didn't want to give her too much information, because I didn't need her getting caught up in my shit. She nodded and turned back over.

I hopped in my rental, and sped back to Embassy Suites hotel. Frank's ass was gone die tonight. I just hoped he wasn't smart enough to skip town overnight, or go to a new hotel. I finally pulled up and made sure I had everything I needed.

I got out the car, and put my hood on. I walked through the lobby, and the night hotel clerks were so into their conversation that they didn't even notice me. When I got onto the elevator, I made sure to look down at my feet so that the camera wouldn't pick up my face. I kept my head down, as I jogged down the second floor hallway to room 212. As I neared the room, I smiled when I heard Frank's voice. He was talking on the phone to someone, and he was crying like the pussy he was.

"They took my baby too, man," he cried. *His baby? This nigga is insane*, I thought.

I wondered how I was gonna be able to get inside his room, then finally just decided to knock. Frank thought he was a fucking G, so he'd answer this door.

"Aye who is it?" he yelled as he neared the door. I didn't respond, and I heard him lean against the door to look through the peephole. "This nigga," he said in a low tone, as I put my silencer on. All of a sudden, after a long pause, the door flung open. "What the fuck you"

PHEW!

PHEW!

PHEW!

There was no need to make conversation or threats. He and I did enough dancing in the past, and he didn't learn then, so he had to get bodied. I jogged back down the hallway, hopped on the elevator and left.

As soon as I got to my hotel, I booked my family a flight back to South Carolina. Hopefully our problems died right along with Greg and Frank.

Lucy was four months pregnant by now, so I was going to visit her. She and Menzo still weren't in a relationship, and it was really stressing her out. I didn't know who to be mad at, because he *did* tell her that they wouldn't progress.

I walked out of the bathroom with just my towel on, and jumped when I saw Menzo standing in the doorway of Julius and I's bedroom.

"Menzo? What are you doing here?"

"Just saying what's up," he smiled seductively.

"Where is Julius?" I asked.

"He's putting some shit in the car. You are so sexy by the way," he bit his lip.

"Thank you?" I replied, as more of a question.

Menzo smiled and turned around to leave. I rushed to the bedroom door, closed it, and then locked it. As soon as I dropped my towel, I heard someone twisting the knob and knocking on the door.

"I'm dressing! Please leave!" I yelled out.

"Natalia, it's me," I heard Julius say.

I picked up my silk robe and walked over to let him in. He walked in and closed the door behind him. He pulled me close, nuzzling his face into my neck.

"You smell good, what is that?" he asked. He frowned up his sexy face, awaiting my response.

"Caress, some brown sugar scent," I smiled.

"No more Herbal Essence?" he chuckled.

"You remembered what kind of soap I liked?" I cocked my head.

"Uh, yeah, you're my lady," he smiled flashing his perfect white teeth. I didn't respond, as I got lost in his stare. "Anyway, I just came to get a kiss goodbye. I will be back around eight, and you, me, and Jackson can go out for dinner."

"Okay, sounds good," I smiled. He grabbed my face and pressed his full lips against mine. My insides became warm, as he grabbed my butt. "Ahh!" I yelped and we laughed in unison.

As soon as he left, I locked the bedroom door and continued to get dressed. It was hot, so I threw on jean shorts, a red tube top, and some brown flip-flops. My brown hair was straightened, so I put it in a low ponytail, with a part down the middle. I put Jackson in a white onesie, dark blue jean shorts, and some brown sandals.

"You're so cute baby," I smiled and pressed my nose against his.

I locked up the house, put the alarm on and headed to Lucy's.

"Let me hold him, with his cute self," Lucy smiled.

"He is such a good baby," Paula smiled as she looked on.

"So far he is, I hope he stays that way," I exhaled.

"Lucy, what's going on with you and" Paula started, but Menzo walked through the door.

"What's up y'all?" he said smiling at me in particular.

I turned away from him, and he laughed. Menzo wasn't tall like Julius, but taller than Lucy and I. He had really nice black hair, which he always wore in a low ponytail. He wore wife beaters every day, just in different colors, with baggy jeans and slide-ins. He was never fresh, in my opinion, like Julius, Rashad, Tim, Dash, and Leese. He was the bottom feeder of the crew, and a part of me wished Lucy hadn't picked him out of what was available.

"We're good," Lucy and Paula said in unison.

"Talia?" he asked. *Talia?*

"I'm good Menzo," I replied dryly.

"Yeah, you look it too," he flirted and walked off. I looked over at Lucy, and she just shook her head.

Once he headed to the back, Paula finished her question for Lucy, in a little bit above a whisper.

"Same shit. He saying we not gone be together, so I'm trying to accept it." Lucy shook her head as a single tear slid down her light face. "I don't know what to do, I should've stayed my ass in Indianapolis." She shook her head again, and looked away.

I took Jackson from her and pulled his bottle out to feed him. I stared at my friend, because I had never seen her this sad before.

"Can we talk about something else?" she finally added after wiping her tears.

"Well Paula, Julius' brother, Rashad likes you," I smiled and so did she.

"So," she chuckled.

"So, can I give him your number?" I asked.

"Uh, I guess. Go ahead," she waved, trying to pretend like she wasn't interested.

"Awwww shit!" Lucy smiled.

"Well, you don't seem too interested, so I won't give it to him," I joked.

"No bitch! You better give him my number!" she frowned and we all laughed. "Nice rock," Paula added.

"Yeah, thank you," I said holding out my hand to look at my engagement ring.

"You think he's actually gonna marry you?" Lucy asked and I nodded. "I hope so," she smiled.

We continued to talk and relax, but I felt so much more comfortable once Menzo left the house.

"Tim and Rashad, the shipment will now need to be picked up at 4am instead of 7am. Cool?" I asked my homeboy and brother.

"I'm cool with that. I be up at that time anyway," my brother Rashad nodded.

"Same," Tim smiled. "Aye, this nigga thirsty!" Tim laughed pointing to Menzo.

"Why what happened?" Dash asked, as we all looked at Menzo.

"Nigga stay liking Natalia's pictures on Instagram dawg," Tim chuckled.

Everyone laughed assuming Menzo was harmless, but it rubbed me the wrong way. Never one to hold my tongue, I decided to speak up.

"Aye, what you liking her pictures for?" I frowned.

"Oh nah man, it ain't even like that. I follow her and she just posts the most." Menzo shrugged.

"Let me see," I said putting my hand out.

"See what?" he frowned.

"See what fucking pictures you liking of my girl nigga!" I boomed and everyone tensed up.

I didn't give a fuck what these niggas thought. I didn't care that they thought this nigga was harmless or meant nothing by his actions. Any nigga that was looking at Natalia had a problem with me, and I didn't give a fuck who he was.

"Man, this some bullshit." Menzo turned his lip up, as he walked his phone over to me.

I snatched his phone from him and went into his likes. I scrolled through the pictures, and like Tim said, 80% of them were of Natalia. Some were of her laughing, making funny faces, or with Lucy or Paula. I had to remind myself that Natalia wasn't gonna be posting sexually suggestive pictures on her Instagram for niggas to drool over.

"Aight, you good," I said sliding his phone across the conference table.

"I know I am. Man, I would never come at Talia like that!" he nodded and smiled. *Talia?*

"Aight, this meeting is adjourned gentlemen, but Menzo, let me holla at you," I said as everyone got up to leave.

"What's up?"

"You like Natalia?" I asked.

"What? Nigga no, she's like a sister to me. Well, sister-in-law," he smiled.

"Good, keep it that way."

<hr>

"I'm so starved!" Natalia said as she looked over the menu.

We decided to go to Friday's for dinner. I kind of wanted to talk to her about Menzo, but I didn't want to seem like some psycho nigga. Fuck it, I *was* psycho when it came to her and my son.

"Baby, has Menzo been acting like he likes you?" I asked.

"Uhm, kind of. Well, I don't know," she replied.

"What has he done?" I questioned.

"He just told me I was beautiful, and then he told me how good I looked when I was over Lucy's," she shrugged.

"Hmm, aight," I replied nodding.

"Are you upset?" she inquired.

"To be honest, kind of. Not with you though ma, but with this nigga."

"I'm sure he didn't mean anything," she smiled.

"Yeah, well let's hope not," I sighed.

Once we were home, Natalia put Jackson to bed and then headed to our room. By the time she walked in, I was already undressed down to my boxers, and lying in bed. She walked over and pulled her tube top over her head. I stared at her sexy ass body, and smiled at my name tatted on her rib cage in small cursive letters. Her small perky breasts, sat up nicely, and my mouth watered as I watched them. She removed her jean shorts, and then grabbed her short nightgown.

"Don't even put that on, come here," I sat up.

She smiled and walked over to the bed, with nothing on. I grabbed her and lay her down in the bed. I kissed her tattoo of my name, and then took her nipples into my mouth. I was addicted to this girl.

Was I interested in Natalia? I most definitely was. It wasn't something I felt as soon as we met, but it grew gradually. The more I saw her around, the sexier she seemed to get. She always had on shorts, showing her nice little ass and sexy caramel legs. Her stomach was nice and flat, and although her breasts weren't big, they were just right. I wanted her, and nine times out of ten, I got what I wanted.

Yeah Julius and I were cool, but why does he get to have it all? He got the drug ring, the money, and now the fine ass girl with a baby. He didn't even appreciate Natalia like I did. He cheated on her constantly, and put his hands on her every chance he got. All that shit about him changing was only gone last for so long. I wasn't gone wait for him to fuck up though, I was just gone show Natalia what the fuck she was missing by being with a nigga like Julius.

Lucy. As far as Lucy, I mean, she was cool and had some great pussy, but Natalia was where it was at. I really didn't want Lucy having my baby, but that was my fault for running up in her hoe ass raw all them damn times. Was I gone be around to raise it? Probably fucking not. I needed to be a father to Jackson, and really wouldn't have any time to help out with Lucy's kid.

"Yeah, right there," I moaned as I looked down at Bianca sucking me up.

Bianca was fine as hell, and the only reason I wanted her was because she was Julius' old girl. See, I promised her ass the world, and since Julius wasn't fucking with her, she became putty in my hands. I'd only been fucking with her for two weeks, and she was already slobbing me up.

"Fuck, here that shit comes," I moaned.

To my fucking surprise, that bitch pulled away making me nut all on my thighs.

"What the fuck you back up for?" I yelled.

"I ain't swallowing your shit nigga!" she turned up her lip.

"Man, whatever. Get yo' ass over here," I frowned. I grabbed her and threw her ass on the bed.

"You got a condom?" Bianca asked as she stood on all fours.

"Nope," I said ramming my dick into her wet pussy.

I reached around and played with her clit, as I pumped into her. Bianca had some fire ass pussy, so I wasn't sure why Julius had drop kicked her. I grabbed onto her waist, and pounded into her shit hard and fast. I closed my eyes, imagining myself thrusting into Natalia's little sexy ass. Not long after I envisioned what her body looked like, I was nutting all up in Bianca.

"Fuck," I moaned.

"I didn't even cum, and you should've pulled out," Bianca whined and rolled her eyes.

"Shut up," I replied pulling a blunt out.

I lit it, and lay down as I took a pull. Bianca crawled up to me, and lay on my chest as I smoked. She took the blunt from me, and then took a pull for herself.

"You know we need to think of something to tell Julius. He gone wonder why I'm in Charleston," she said.

"Fuck what Julius is wondering! He needs to worry about his own bitch, not mine," I spat.

"So I'm your bitch?" she smiled and laughed like it was a joke.

"You know you are," I smirked. She knew what it was though. She was hoping my plans to break up Natalia and Julius worked, so she could have him.

"What about Lucy?" she inquired.

"She just another hoe claiming to be having my baby," I lied. I knew damn well Lucy's baby was mine, but if I denied it long enough, maybe it would somehow become go away.

"Good," she said sitting up.

I put the blunt out, as Bianca climbed up to sit on my face. I pulled her clit into my mouth, and sucked the life out of her.

"Yes, eat this pussy daddy. Fuck," she moaned as I cupped her ass cheeks.

Just as she started to ride my face, I closed my eyes and envisioned Natalia's sweet pussy in my mouth.

2 WEEKS LATER

It was my eighteenth birthday tonight, and Julius decided to throw me a big party at this venue called Club Rissani. It was a nice venue, with a Moroccan theme. I only knew about it because Julius had shown me pictures. It was new in town, and was for an over 21 crowd only, so I wasn't sure how I was able to host my birthday there. Julius just said *your nigga is the man around here, that's all you need to know.* I laughed as I thought about what he said. I'd never had a birthday party before, so I was really excited for it. Julius said he had a lot of surprises for me tonight, and I couldn't wait.

I hired a babysitter for Jackson, and made sure she was no fuck buddy of Julius' beforehand. She was a really sweet older lady name Winifred, who agreed to take care of Jackson whenever I needed it. I made sure that Julius paid her well, because she was so helpful all the time.

"Okay Winnie, did you need anything before I leave?" I asked my babysitter.

"Nope, we are good. You look beautiful Natalia!" she smiled as she walked over for a hug. I had on a yellow maxi dress, by For Love & Lemons. It was a yellow embroidery material, from my collarbone to right under my butt cheeks. The rest of the dress was see-through lace material, with a split down the middle. I wore some beige Red Bottom stilettoes that wrapped around my ankle. My hair was straightened, with loose body waves all over.

"Thank you," I smiled. I walked over to Jackson, and gave him a light peck on his fat cheek.

Just as I was walking down the steps of the condo, I heard a loud car horn. When I walked outside, it was a black Bentley and a driver waiting, just like in Los Angeles. I smiled as I neared the car, and the driver opened the door.

"Happy Birthday Natalia," the driver smiled.

"Thank you," I replied as he helped me into the car.

When I got into the car, I noticed a bottle of pink champagne. I remembered telling Julius I always wanted to try it, because it was so pretty. It appeared to be just opened, because a smoke of some sort was coming out of the top.

"Happy Birthday baby girl, enjoy," read the note attached.

I smiled and poured myself a glass. I sipped the drink and listened to music, as we rode to Club Rissani. Once we pulled up, there was a long line of people outside. There were bouncers and red ropes every-where. The club looked like an Arabian castle; it was the most beautiful thing I'd ever seen. *We have to be at the wrong place, this can't all be for me,* I thought. I finished off my glass of champagne, just as the driver opened the door. A red carpet ran from the door of the Bentley, to the front double doors of the club. The driver helped me exit the car and walked me up to the bouncer.

"Happy Birthday Natalia!" a couple people yelled, and I just smiled 'cause I didn't know who they were.

The bouncer told me happy birthday, then took the rope down, and moved to the side for me to walk in. I walked in, and there was a big sign above the club reading *Happy Birthday Natalia*. I smiled, and looked around the huge club. It was packed and everyone was getting their freak on to "Thought It Was a Drought" by Future.

"Happy Birthday baby," I heard a familiar voice say. I looked up and saw Julius. He looked so good in a blood red colored suit, with a white button up. He wore a red bowtie, and his wrists were iced out as usual.

"Thank you daddy," I smiled as he kissed me. "How did you get all this for me?" I asked again.

"This is my club. I've been having it built since I lived in Indianapolis," he winked.

Two bodyguards escorted us up to the VIP area, where I spotted Lucy, Paula, and to my surprise, Victoria. Tim, Dash, Rashad, Leese, and unfortunately Menzo, were all there as well. I hugged everyone except Menzo, and then lightly jogged to Victoria.

"What are you doing here?" I smiled.

"Your baby daddy flew me out," she smiled and smacked her lips. I hugged her again, and then we started to party.

"Flex" by Rich Homie Quan was blasting, and everybody was dancing their asses off. I had never had this much fun in my entire life. It was also the first time I'd seen Lucy smile in a long time. I did catch Menzo sitting on the velvet couch, staring at me with a smile on his face. I thanked God that Julius was here to protect me, if he tried anything.

"All Eyes On You" by Meek Mill started to play, and I smiled at Julius 'cause that was our favorite song. I was sitting on his lap, as we rapped the words to one another. I looked over and spotted Rashad and Paula looking super cozy. I made a mental note to ask her about that.

Around 2am, Julius and I decided to leave. Paula walked up to me and handed me a wrapped gift before I left. I thanked her then said bye to everyone. Just as I was walking down the steps holding Julius' hand, Menzo stopped me to hand me another gift.

"From me and Lucy," he smiled. "Y'all have a goodnight," he added as he slowly walked backwards into the VIP area.

"Thank you for watching him Winnie. The guest bedroom is ready for you." I smiled at her and she hugged me.

"For you," she smiled and handed me a keychain. It was a multicolored crocheted baseball. It had the words Guatemala, her home, sewed into it.

"This is beautiful Winnie, thank you," I smiled and she nodded.

I walked into Julius and my bedroom, and started to undress. I heard the shower running, so I knew Julius was in there. I opened the gift from Paula, which was a Starbucks gift card. She knew I loved their iced teas, and that this would be perfect for me. I then grabbed the gift that Menzo handed me. I wondered why Lucy didn't give it to me herself. I took it out the bag, and saw it was a blue box with a white ribbon. There was a note attached to it that read: *I love you. Happy birthday.* I quickly threw it back in the bag and opened the box. It was a silver bead bracelet from Tiffany's. I admired the beautiful bracelet, until I heard the shower water stop. I quickly closed the blue box, and put it in my panty drawer.

Julius walked out and smiled at me. He kissed my lips, and then went to put on some boxers, basketball shorts, and a t-shirt. He went over to his closet, and then grabbed two big bags out.

"Here is the first of your gifts," he said, handing it to me.

I opened the big bag, and saw a Jimmy Choo shoebox. I opened the first one, and spotted the red Lilyth 120 shoes that I'd wanted. I never mentioned it to Julius though, so I wasn't sure how he knew to buy them. I sat them down and grabbed the Louboutin shoebox. I opened them to see the Bobsleigh boots in beige.

"Oh my gosh Julius!" I beamed as I tried both shoes on.

"I told you it was gonna be different once I started making some real money," he reminded me.

I then realized there were two more Louboutin boxes. I opened them to see the two colorful pumps I had been looking at. They were called Pigalle Follies or something like that.

"How did you know I wanted these shoes?" I asked as I looked at them in the mirror.

"Easy. You fell asleep every night with your iPad open. You had all of them up on your browser tabs. After doing that a couple nights, I realized you really wanted them," he chuckled.

This Julius was nothing like the man I met at CVS, and I loved it. He was still rough around the edges, and didn't take any shit, but this Julius was in love with me just like I'd always been with him. I was so lucky to have him, and I was glad I stuck around.

"Aight, one more," he smiled and grabbed my hand.

He led me to the garage, and placed his hand over my eyes. I laughed for no reason, wondering what the hell was going on. We finally stopped, and he removed his hand. It was a silver BMW X5 with a big red bow on the hood.

"What is this?" I asked.

"Your car ma," he smirked.

"Oh my gosh, Julius, this is..." I was speechless as I looked over the car.

"And I won't take this one back. I promise," he added.

He handed me the keys, and I hopped inside to take a quick look. I saw he already had Jackson's car seat strapped into it. I got out after a while, and ran into his arms. He then carried me upstairs so we could make love. I made sure to keep on my red Lilyth heels while we did too.

"Damn Nat," Julius moaned as I bounced on his dick.

I had my back to him, riding him backwards. He smacked and grabbed my ass, making me cum hard.

"Julius… ahhh," I whimpered as I shivered lightly.

He leaned me back, and then got between my legs. He placed my legs on his arms, where we could both see my beautiful shoes. He thrust into me, as he sucked on my nipples.

"Fuck babe," he groaned.

He let my legs down, and pinned my hands above my head. He sped up, beating my pussy up, and making me cum hard as hell.

"You're so fucking sexy. Damn," he grunted as he kissed my neck and jaw line. He dipped his tongue in my mouth, and continued to make love to me throughout the night. This was the best birthday ever.

JULIUS

I was leaving the construction site for Natalia and my new house. I was starting to feel like the condo was too small, plus it was only meant to be temporary anyway. We needed a house, where we could have more room and rooms. This new house I was having built, had six bedrooms, five bathrooms, not including the his and hers in the master bedroom, two offices, a gym, a backyard with a tennis court, pool, and Jacuzzi, two dens, a spacious foyer, two dining rooms, and a huge ass kitchen. I only wanted five bedrooms at first, but Natalia wanted Winnie to move in with us as well.

"It's looking good guys, when do you think it will all be done?" I asked my contractor Clayton.

Yes my contractor. Anything I was having built, was being done by him and his people. He was responsible for construction of Club Rissani, and he did a wonderful job. Currently I had him working on my house, and my brother Rashad had him working on his. I paid Clayton well, and always made sure to provide lunches and dinners for he and his crew. Clayton was an older black guy, and I always looked out for my own people. Don't get me wrong though, Clayton deserved the job.

"Just give us three more months buddy, and you guys can move in.

We will be done in two months, but we want to make sure everything is perfect before you and Mrs. Tate move in," he replied and I nodded.

"Aight well, sounds like a plan. I'll see y'all tomorrow." I said.

I hopped in my car, because I had a meeting to go to. These young niggas wanted to meet with me, in hopes of getting some work. All I really needed was some more people working the blocks, because it seemed like we didn't have enough people to match the demand. The last thing I needed was a bunch of base heads hanging around my traps, waiting to be serviced. That would only bring unwanted attention, and that unwanted attention would be from the police.

My phone chimed, and I saw it was a text from Franceska. She had been blowing me up for well over a month, and I'd been ignoring her. I was really trying to do right by my girl, and I knew Franceska would make that hard for me. I mean, the girl went as far as to have my damn name tatted.

Franceska: I miss you Ju.

Me: Franceska stop. I'm gone be married soon, and I ain't tryna get into nothing with you. Peace.

Franceska: Oh now you wanna be faithful? I swear I can't stand yo flip flopping ass Ju! You got your dick in my mouth one day, and then you tryna be a family man the next. Fuck you.

Me: Keep talking slick Franceska. Don't hit me up no more.

Franceska: Ju, baby. Don't do me like this!

I just shook my head and deleted the conversation. I promised myself and my girl that I was gone be on the straight and narrow. It was a promise to my son too, because I know how much I hated to see my mom's boyfriend dog her out. I'm sure if Jackson were older, he wouldn't want his mother being mistreated, especially by his own father.

Franceska: I'm still in Charleston. I decided to stay.

I didn't respond, and placed my phone back in the cup holder.

By now, my office was completely finished, and it looked like one of those insurance offices. I made sure it looked legit, because I didn't need any pigs sniffing around any of my shit. Plus, majority of my income appeared to be clean due to my movie theater investments and newly - Club Rissani. I pulled into the parking lot around back, and then walked into the glass building. The security guards nodded to say what's up as I walked by.

At the advice of Bart, I had two security scanners by the door. Badges had to be scanned in order to get by. If your badge was revoked, the alarms would beep and security would escort you out. Bart said it was a good way to keep niggas who went from friends to enemies out, and I agreed. I headed to my office, and spotted the two little niggas I was supposed to meet. I wore a short-sleeved DOPE denim chaos button up, Zara jeans, black Nike Roshe sneakers, and a black snapback.

"What's up y'all?" I asked as I sat down.

Dash and Leese, sat on each opposite end of my office, making sure nothing went wrong prior to me walking in. They decided to stay in case these niggas had something up their sleeve.

"What's up Julius!" the two young guys said as they stood to dap me up.

"Y'all can relax, y'all a bit tense," I commented.

"My bad homie, we just heard some things," one replied and half smiled.

"Like what?"

"That you were ruthless," the other added.

"Well, when it comes to my business and my money, yeah I am ruthless. But anyway, what's y'all names?" I asked.

I wanted niggas to respect me, not fear me. Fear is what caused niggas to retaliate and plan against you; respect kept niggas loyal. I was in no way scared of Hugo when I worked for him, but I respected him, until he dogged me, which meant much more.

"I'm Luke."

"Jabari," the other replied.

"Nice to meet y'all," I said, as my assistant, Deirdre brought in some drinks for everybody.

Deirdre was Clayton's wife. See, when I met them, they were a half an inch away from losing their home. Clayton was laid off from a good construction job for the sixth time, and Deirdre was fired from a call center. They had three kids, and needed money bad, so I employed them both.

"Likewise," Luke and Jabari said in unison.

"So, do y'all know anything about working traps?" I questioned.

"Yeah, well kind of. We worked for this one cat named Brax. He was like the king of Charleston before he got locked up," Luke started.

"Brax was making a lot of bread, but not as much as you Julius. When he got locked up, we vowed to never get back in the game, but my moms needs help paying bills so I need to do something about it. Shit, I'm 23 years old, and McDonalds ain't cutting it. The way you run shit is smooth as hell, and we feel comfortable and safe working for you," Jabari added, and I liked what I heard.

"So y'all hungry, huh?" I smirked.

"We are, and I promise you we can do it," Jabari replied.

"Well, we get a lot of business, like a whole lot. Now if you can handle keeping customers from hanging around the traps, possibly defending yourself against fuck niggas and holding your own, then this is for you. Like you said Jabari, this is a smooth running business. It runs just like a legit factory, and in order to keep it that way, we need to have the right people," I said and they both nodded. "Obviously, I will supply y'all with heat if anything were to go down, but you need to be able to handle shit yourselves sometimes," I said.

See, I was like that store manager that had been a cashier before. The managers that worked their way up were much better managers than the ones who just started as a manager. I had been everything a young street nigga could be. I was a stick up kid at fourteen, worked traps from age fifteen to seventeen, and then Hugo put me on to bigger shit after that. So I definitely worked my way up the street ladder.

"Aight, so meet me back here tomorrow. I'm gone do a little background check on y'all. You know, ask around and make sure y'all loyal. Because if there is anything that will make me put a bullet in you, it would be disloyalty. So by 12pm tomorrow, be here, and my brother Rashad is gon' show you how shit works in my traps. Now listen to how I said *my* traps. My shit works different than the shit you used to, I'm sure of it," I said.

"I'm ready man, and I promise you ain't gone hear shit about us that you don't like. You got some loyal niggas right here," Luke nodded and smiled. Dash, Leese, and I all chuckled.

"Good, good. Aye, are y'all brothers or something? Y'all seem to be tight as hell," I asked.

"Cousins," Jabari replied and smiled.

"Aight well, cheers to that!" I said and held my glass up.

Jabari, Luke, Dash, Leese, and I talked a little bit more, just so I could get to know who I might possibly be dealing with on a more personal level. Franceska blew me up the whole damn time, to the point where I had to block her ass. These hoes were really acting up.

NATALIA

1 WEEK LATER

Me: *Outside.*

I text Paula to let her know I was here. She usually drove everywhere, but since I had a new car courtesy of my love, I wanted to drive. We were gonna go get our nails and hair done. This trip was much needed, and plus I wanted to talk to her about Menzo. I didn't want to talk to Lucy yet, because I didn't want to start anything. Telling Lucy was like telling Julius. I knew Julius would heat up the city if he knew another guy was trying to pursue me.

"Hey cutie," Paula said to Jackson, as she buckled her 4-year-old daughter, Gabby in. Jackson just made some baby noises, making her and me chuckle. "And hey to you beautiful," Paula said as she slid into the front seat, giving me a hug.

"How are you?" I asked pulling away from the curb.

"I'm actually doing good as hell," she smiled.

"Is it because of Rashad?" I smiled while keeping my eyes on the road.

"Enh, maybe," she chuckled.

"I already know it is." I shook my head.

"Yeah, I'm usually not into the thug types, but I'm really feeling Rashad," she smiled as she stared out the window.

"Paula has a boo, I thought I'd never see the day," I chuckled.

"Whatever bitch," she snickered.

After we got our hair and nails done, we decided to go have a little evening lunch at Red Lobster. I was craving some crab legs, and Paula wanted some of their famous Parmesan pasta.

"I looveee strawberry lemonade." I smiled as I sipped my drink.

"Yes, we know crazy," Paula laughed.

Her daughter, Gabby was sitting next to her across from me, and Jackson was in his little car seat/carrier with the cover pulled down, sitting next to me. I was so happy that he fell asleep. I fed him a bottle in the parking lot, and he passed right out.

I decided now was a good time to discuss Menzo, since little Gabby was occupied with the color sheet and crayons the waitress had given her. I simply slid my iPhone across the table, with the texts from Menzo on full display. He had somehow obtained my number, and was now sending me texts all the time.

"What the fuck?" she frowned as she slowly scrolled through the texts.

Menzo: Have a good night babe.

Me: Who is this?

Menzo: Your future ma.

Me: Who?

Menzo: Menzo.

No reply.

Menzo: Good morning babe, hope you're having a good day.

Menzo: No reply? It's cool, I know you probably busy with the lil man.

Menzo: Did you like the bracelet I bought?

"What bracelet?" Paula looked up at me.

"He got me a bracelet from Tiffany's for my birthday," I replied. She shook her head and continued reading.

Menzo: Those lips. I stay on your Instagram ma.

Me: Menzo please stop texting me.

Menzo: Whatever, in due time ma.

"What the fuck Nat? Have you told Lucy?" Paula asked sliding my phone back to me.

"No, I didn't want to upset her. But I guess I should, huh?"

"Uh, hell yeah, she's thinking they're a couple. Well never mind, she says he's telling her they're not," she replied.

"I just don't want Julius to do anything crazy," I said as the waitress set our food down.

"Yeah that's true. Maybe just show Lucy, and tell her not to say anything around Julius or to Julius," Paula suggested and I nodded.

Paula and I parted ways after a nice dinner, and I couldn't stop thinking about telling Lucy. She was almost full term, and I didn't want to stress her out. But like Paula said, she needed to know what Menzo was up to.

After I pulled into the garage, I pulled out my phone to call Lucy. I decided to tell her what was going on over the phone, 'cause I couldn't bear to look at her face.

"Hey boo," she answered.

"Hey, how are you feeling?" I asked.

"I'm ready for this little boy to be out," she replied.

"A boy? What are you gonna name him?" I inquired.

"Menzo Jr.," she replied, and reminded me why I was calling in the first place.

"Lucy, I wanted to talk to you about Menzo. He's been flirting with me a lot."

"Menzo is just joking. He plays like that," she said.

"Are you sure? Because he bought me a bracelet, and he's telling me he"

"Can you take me to my appointment tomorrow?" she asked changing the subject. I paused for a moment because I was confused.

"Okay. What time?" I questioned.

"11:30am. Thanks," she quickly replied and disconnected the call.

I exhaled heavily, and then exited the car. I slowly walked up the stairs, and was surprised to see Julius lying in bed watching TV. I was happy he was home this early. Although it was 10pm, that was early for Julius.

"Hey baby girl," he smiled as I walked in.

I stripped down to my white thong panties, and nothing else. I climbed in bed as Julius stared at me seductively. I kissed his lips, and then collapsed on my stomach; I just wanted to go to sleep. He leaned down, and then smacked and bit my butt cheek.

"Ow!" I whined and chuckled.

He pulled my thong to the side, and started to suck on my clit from the back. He spread my cheeks some more, and sucked harder until I came.

"Ahhh Julius. Damn," I moaned.

As I lay there on my stomach, he climbed over me. He grabbed my thong and tugged it down roughly. He lifted me up, so that my ass was tooted in the air.

"Look at that pretty shit," he commented, as he bent down and ran his tongue along my vagina.

"Oooh," I whispered in a low tone, as if I was cold.

"Spread your legs wider for daddy," he commanded.

I did as I was told, and I felt his tongue go in my ass. He was sucking from my clit all the way up to my ass, and it was driving me crazy. After cumming two more times, Julius positioned himself under me.

"Ride my face," he said.

I was spent, but I knew my baby wouldn't take no for an answer. I sat down on his face, and he pulled my swollen clit back into his mouth. He put his hands under my thighs, and lifted them up. I leaned back some, and propped myself up on his bottom half. I slowly wound my hips, as he sucked the life out of my pussy.

"Oh God! Julius. Mmmmm, uhhh," I cried loud as hell.

I knew Winnie could hear us, but as good as this was feeling, I didn't care. I tucked my lips in, as I felt a tear slide down my face. My pelvis tensed up, and my body jerked, as I exploded into his mouth. I pulled away, and Julius made a pop sound with his mouth, that made me moan so fucking loud.

"That shit tastes good baby," he whispered and bit his lip.

I turned over on all fours, and tried to crawl away. Julius rushed me from behind, and licked and bit my shoulder, making me cry out in pleasure. He wrapped his strong arm around my mid-section, and sucked on my neck. He spread my legs with his knees, and then wiggled his long, thick manhood into my pussy from behind.

"Juuu, ahhh baby," I whined as he stroked me from behind.

I collapsed forward, and he went right down with me, continuing to thrust into me.

"Fuck, you feel so good," he panted, as he craned his neck around to suck on my lips. He slid his hand down the front of my body and played with my clit. "Look how wet you get for daddy," he whispered as he sucked on my shoulders.

Although this was the only dick I knew, I was sure it was the fucking best there ever was. He pulled me back up, and grabbed a handful of my hair. He thrust into me, and the sound of how wet I was could be heard throughout the house for sure. I spread my legs some more, and started slowly throwing it back.

"Yes, baby girl, just like that," Julius grunted.

I looked over my shoulder, and saw him watching his dick go in and out of me. He sped up some, and we both started yelling loud as hell. *Poor Winnie.* I thought. My muscles tightened around his rod, so I knew I was about to cum.

"Look at daddy when you cum," he said in a low tone.

I looked at him over my shoulder, and we locked eyes as we both exploded. He slowly pumped into me, releasing everything in him, and then flipped me over. He climbed between my legs and tongued me down. He sucked on my nipples softly, and then kissed back up to my lips. We fell asleep just like that.

LUCY OUISTIN

I stared at the clock, which read 10:30am, and I knew Natalia would be here in about twenty minutes. I was laid on my back with my legs cocked open, as Menzo pumped away. I could barely get into it, as Natalia's and my conversation replayed in my mind.

"Arrggghhh," Menzo grunted as he released into me.

He fell to the side, and I immediately hopped up off the bed. I grabbed my toiletries, and then headed to the bathroom. I scrubbed myself feverishly in the shower, trying to remove the scent of Menzo from my body. I hated him at this point, but felt the need to stay for my baby. I washed my face to remove any traces of tears, and then got out to get dressed.

I threw on a simple sundress and some sandals. Just as I finished putting my medium-length, dark hair in a low ponytail, my phone buzzed. I reached for it, but Menzo snatched it up.

"Where you and Natalia going?" he frowned after reading it.

"To my doctor's appointment that you said you couldn't make, remember?" I asked snatching my phone back from him.

"Man, calm yo' ass down aight!" he yelled.

"Whatever Menzo, and I better not find out you got a thing for Natalia!" I spat.

"And if you do?" he raised a brow.

"I'm gone tell Julius nigga," I replied and turned to leave.

Before I could hit the door, I felt Menzo grab a fistful of my hair. He yanked me back and slammed the bedroom door.

"Stop Menzo! What the fuck!" I screamed.

"You bet not say shit to Julius! If I even think you talking to him, I'll perform a back alley abortion on yo' ass while you're asleep!" he said through gritted teeth, as he tightened his grip on my hair. My freshly done ponytail was fucked up for sure.

"Okay, okay," I begged as I felt like my scalp was bleeding.

As soon as he let me go, I wobbled out of the house and into Natalia's car. As soon as she pulled off, I burst into tears. I hated my life right about now, and ending it seemed like the best thing to do.

"What's wrong Lucy?" Natalia tried to rub my back, and drive at the same time.

"Nothing, nothing, I'm good." I shook my head and wiped my tears.

Out the corner of my eye, I could see her staring at me for as long she could, while still trying to drive. I turned the radio up, and then stared out the window the rest of the way. Christina Milian's "Gonna Tell Everybody" played through the speakers, and the lyrics made my eyes water again.

How could I let this situation get the best of me, when I gave the best of me? It's just crazy, how one minute we connect; I was baby, your lady, sweet Sadie, holding hands was your favorite. Now I, ain't got no sad song to sing, 'cause youse dead wrong to me, 'cause I was so committed.

The words resonated with me, and I closed my eyes to let the tears fall. Before I knew it, we'd arrived at the doctor's office

---

I was sitting in the office of my doctor. We already did the check up in the patient room, but she said she wanted to talk to me about some other things. I asked for Natalia to stay out in the waiting room, because I was sure there was a problem. I hadn't been feeling well in some areas, but I needed my doctor to confirm it.

"Sorry about that little wait, Lucy, my assistant needed help with the new program we just got," my doctor said as she sat behind her desk.

"It's okay," I shrugged as I rubbed my sweaty palms together.

"Okay," she said breathily, as she opened a couple file folders. "We did see that you had an STI honey, so I will give you something to take for that. How many partners do you have?"

"Just one at the moment," I replied.

"Is this the father of your baby?" she asked.

"Yes, he is," I nodded.

"Okay, well you need to make sure he goes and gets treated as well. Are you familiar with the ping pong effect?" she asked and I shook my head no. "That is when one partner treats a disease, but the other partner doesn't, before they engage in sexual activity again and then vice versa. So for example, if you take your pills for the chlamydia that you tested positive for today, and then go have sex with your child's father before he gets treated, you'll have the STI again. Then after he gets treated by his doctor, he is gonna come home and sleep with you, where he will catch it again. So you guys start this thing, where you're bouncing it back to each other like a ping-pong game. Make sense?"

"Yes, I understand," I replied. I was so furious with Menzo, and just depressed at the same time.

"Okay honey. Well let me write the prescription that you can pick up from your preferred pharmacy. Take it as soon as possible, and remember, do not have sex with your son's father until he gets treated, and until you can verify that he has been." She stared into my eyes to let me know she meant business, and I nodded.

"So what happened in her office?" Natalia asked as we pulled out of the Wendy's driveway.

As I was about to speak, her phone chimed four times back to back. I snatched it up before she could, and saw she had two texts from Menzo, one from Paula, and one from Julius.

"What's your passcode?" I asked.

"Julius and I agreed not to have passcodes," she responded without looking at me.

I slid open her phone, and went straight to her texts. I clicked the one Julius had sent, just out of curiosity first.

Boyfriend: *I love you too.*

I scrolled up and saw she was telling him she loved him and missed him. I shook my head and smiled, then backed out.

"What is it Lucy?" Natalia asked.

I ignored her, and clicked the text from Menzo, which I could already see a preview of. I closed my eyes, and took a deep breath before reading it.

Menzo: *I wanna make love to you.*

Menzo: *Just let me make love to you once ma, and I will leave you alone.*

I scrolled up, and saw he text her constantly with things similar to the one I'd just read. I wanted to be mad at Natalia too, but I couldn't. She'd only responded once, telling him to leave her alone.

"Lucy!" Natalia yelled as she stopped in front of Menzo's condo.

"What?" I frowned.

"I tried to tell you," she said referring to Menzo.

"Why, so you could rub it in my face Natalia?!"

"No Lucy, so you could know what type of guy he is," she replied.

"What about the type of nigga you got? Oh, you think 'cause he promised to be faithful to you for a fucking month out of the year that you got something good? The way he used to cheat on you, beat you up, and then disregard your ass for weeks at a time! And let's not forget the abortion he forced on your dumb ass! Yet you have the nerve to talk about my nigga?!" I yelled. When I looked over at her, tears were running down her face. "Nat, I-I'm sorry I didn't mean any of that. I'm just acting jealous becau"

"Just get out Lucy. I need to get home," she cut in while looking straight ahead.

"Okay. I'm sorry Nat, I love you," I said staring at the side of her beautiful face. "Here," I finally said, handing her the phone before I hopped out.

I walked up the stairs, replaying the things I'd just said to only person who'd ever cared about me. I hated to be mean to my best friend, but the truth is, I hated her right now. I was jealous that a man we all thought would never change had changed for little old Natalia. The thing I loved about my best friend was something I also hated. She was simple and never tried hard, but that always drew people to her. She was nothing like the girls that were voted most popular, but the popular guys always wanted her. Guys like Julius seemed to love her. It made me feel a little bit good when I saw how badly Julius was treating her. I thought, for once, she understands how it feels to have a broken heart. For once, she finally hasn't been able to capture a man's heart. For once, a man is treating her badly, and doesn't like her as much. I celebrated all too soon, as Julius began to fall for her, and now the man I hoped would change for me, has too. I loved Natalia more than Tia loved Tamara, but her effortless perfection annoyed me to the core. Her ability to make Julius fall in love with her without chasing him, scheming on him, or beating up any bitch he came in contact with, irked my soul. However, I won't allow my jealousy and low self-esteem to hurt the only person who has ever cared enough about me, to make sure I ate ever day and had good clothes to wear, when she barely had those things herself.

Me: *I'm sorry Natalia. I love you. Please forgive me.*

"Back already?" Menzo asked as he turned up a beer, while watching TV.

"You know you gave me chlamydia?"

"You a got damn lie bitch!" he yelled standing up.

"I can't do this anymore with you Menzo!" I yelled through tears.

"You can't do what? You ain't going no fucking where!"

"Why do you even want me here?! You're in love with Natalia!" I screamed as if I was terrified of every word that just left my lips.

"Well until I get her, you all I fucking got! Now sit yo' ass down!" he said through gritted teeth.

I did as I was told, and cried for what seemed like forever. Menzo watched basketball and pretended not to hear me, until he went upstairs to bed.

JULIUS

I t was about 3am, when I finally got home. I was tired as hell, and starting to think I needed some sort of vacation. I was thinking maybe Natalia and I should go and get married somewhere, now that she was eighteen years old. I knew with her is where I wanted to be, so I might as well marry her pretty ass.

I felt grimy, so I wanted to take a nice hot shower before climbing into bed with baby girl. I walked up the stairs towards our bedroom, and thought about the fact that we'd be in our new house in two more months. I wanted to be married by the time we got in it though. I laughed at my thoughts, because before I met Natalia, and even a little after I met her, I never saw myself getting married or falling in love.

As I neared the room, I heard light sniffles. I walked to Jackson's room first, to make sure he was okay. I let out a sigh of relief to know that Natalia wasn't crying over something that happened to him. I peeked into Winnie's room and saw she was watching TV.

"Did you need something Mr. Tate?" she smiled and stepped halfway out of the bed.

"Nah, no, just making sure everyone is okay."

I headed back to the bedroom to see what was wrong with Natalia. I walked in and saw she had the covers pulled over her head. Her body was jerking lightly, as she sobbed hard as fuck. I walked closer, and kneeled down next to her bed.

"Baby what's wrong?" I asked as I peeled the covers back.

Her pretty face was wet with tears, and her pouty full lips were red. I wiped a couple tears away with my thumb and kissed her.

"What's wrong Natalia?" I asked again.

"Do you really l-love me?" she sniffled.

"Yeah baby girl, you know I do," I said climbing into the bed with her.

"Yo-you haven't been with any other girls?"

"Nah, not since I promised you," I replied squinting. "Why babe?"

"Just making sure," she finally smiled.

I figured now was the perfect time to see if she wanted to get married, since for some reason she was questioning my love for her.

"What you think about getting married in two months?"

"For real?"

"Yeah, for real. So what you think?" I asked kissing the back of her hand.

"Okay," she chuckled and I kissed her lips.

I continued to kiss her soft lips, until I was in between her soft legs; my favorite place.

***

I was hungry as fuck, so I decided to stop at Subway to get something to eat. As I stood in line, I felt like someone was staring at me. Just as I suspected, I looked to my left to see Franceska watching me like a hawk. *What the fuck?* She was like a leech that I couldn't get rid of. I proceeded to stand in line and order my sandwich, while not paying attention to her. On my way out, she decided to finally speak up.

"Ju!" she called after me.

Just like before, I kept walking all the way until I reached my Audi. I hit my alarm and put my sandwich inside, in case she wanted to get crazy. If she made me drop my sandwich I may have to lay her ass out in broad daylight.

"Juli"

"What Franceska?" I asked folding my arms.

"So that's it. You tell me you gone try to be faithful and that's it?" she cried throwing her arms out.

"Oh my fucking gosh man," I said rubbing my hand over my face. "In your perfect world Franceska, what would you want from me?"

"For you to love me like I love you."

"Okay. But you do realize that I have someone and that isn't gonna change ma. But even if there was no Natalia, you and I wouldn't work."

"Why? 'Cause I'm only good enough to fuck!" she yelled.

"Bring your damn voice down, and in my eyes, yes. That's all I see you for. You need to find a nigga that's gone want to be with you outside the bedroom, 'cause it ain't me," I shrugged.

"You gone regret those words Julius," she glared at me.

"Don't come at me with threats ma, you don't want that with me," I replied and hopped in my car.

I sped out the parking lot, and left her standing there with her arms folded. I prayed that this would be the last time I ever heard from her ass. Hopefully, she would move back to Indiana and move on with her life.

I really didn't know what the fuck Julius thought this was. I mean, I got this nigga's name tatted between my breasts! We been fucking around for almost a year now, and he never gave a fuck about Natalia any of those times. When I met his ass he was fucking with Natalia, Bianca, and a whole other slew of bitches, so I don't understand why I'm not making the cut.

I had two plans in mind though, and they would definitely work out for me one way or the other. I'd been watching Julius and Natalia for a week now, and I felt it'd be a good time to let his little wifey know what kind of dirty ass nigga she had on her hands.

I smiled when I saw Natalia pull up in front of her condo. She got out the car, and an older lady grabbed her son out the back, as she popped the trunk. She started taking groceries in and out of her condo, and when I saw she was closing the trunk, I got out and ran over to her.

"Natalia!" I called out, hoping to stop her from walking away.

"Lisa," she said nonchalantly, and rolled her eyes. *Bitch!* I forgot I had given her a fake name when I applied to work for her.

"I wanted to talk to you," I smiled.

"About what?" she quizzed folding her arms.

"About Julius. I have some stuff you may want to know. Can we go inside and talk?" I smiled.

"No, tell me right here," she replied catching me off guard.

"O-okay… well, Julius and I have been sleeping together, pretty much as long as you guys have been together." I raised a brow.

"Oh, yeah. You're old news though," she replied calmly.

"Is that what you think? Well did you know about"

"The hotel threesome," she laughed.

"No, last night we fucked until 3am," I had to lie.

"That's funny, because I'm pretty sure he and I were fucking until about 5am." She smiled and turned around to leave.

I stood there for a couple seconds, and then finally walked away. It was time for plan B; one that I knew for sure would pull them apart.

I sped to Club Rissani, where I knew Julius would be around this time of the day. I spotted his car in the employee parking lot in the back, and got out of my car. I dug through my purse, and dropped a nice amount of drugs on the floor in his backseat. His window was cracked, so it was easy to slide these little baggies through. I had everything from weed, cocaine, to pills and meth. Once I was done, I sprinted back to my car, and made the call.

"Charleston PD," a man answered.

"Hi, yes. I would like to report a young man by the name of Julius Tate. He's been distributing drugs around town, and I wanted to let someone know," I smiled.

"Do you have a good location for Mr. Tate?" the man answered.

"Yes, his black Audi RS 7, is parked in the back of Rissani night club right now," I replied and gave them his plate number.

"Thanks for the tip, we will be right over," the officer said and we disconnected.

About fifteen minutes later, I saw two police cars pull up. One officer hopped out of each, and they headed towards the back parking lot. I watched as they shined a flashlight into Julius' car to look around. One of the officers spotted what I planted, and shook his head. They turned around and headed over to the entrance of the club. It was around 2pm, so the doors were locked. They beat on the door and waited. Finally, some young man answered the door that I didn't recognize. They spoke a couple words to him, and then he went back inside. A couple minutes later, Julius came to the door. The officers tugged him out and threw handcuffs on him. I laughed to myself, and wanted to jump up and down as they escorted him to the police car.

Once they were gone, I sped back to his condo to watch the drama unfold. Not but twenty minutes later, I saw little smart mouth ass Natalia running outside to get in her BMW truck, and sped off. I smiled and decided to treat myself to a nice lunch for a job well done.

It seemed as if my worst nightmare was coming true. Julius had gotten locked up for possession of illegal drugs. He called me to let me know that I needed to go pick up his brother and stop by his lawyer's house. I immediately ran outside and headed to get Rashad.

"Okay, so where do I go?" I asked Rashad frantically.

"Relax ma, Ju gone be aight," he said rubbing my back and I nodded.

He gave me directions on how to get to Julius' lawyer, Benjamin's house, as he talked on the phone with him. I was going as fast as I could, 'cause for some reason I thought the faster I drove, the quicker Julius would be out.

We pulled up to a nice two-story house, and Benjamin was already walking out. He waved his hands for us to come in quickly.

"Benjamin Brown," he said sticking his hand out to me, once I walked in.

"Natalia," I smiled and sat down next to Rashad.

"Okay, so I made some calls after talking to you Rashad, and it looks like they found a lot of shit in Julius' back seat. I've never known Julius to be that reckless," he started the conversation.

"He ain't, we already know someone set him up, but we don't know who," Rashad shook his head.

"Right, now I know Julius didn't put those there, so we need to find out who did. I ordered to have the fingerprints on the bags of drugs scanned. That will tell us who at least touched the drugs last, which we know is not Julius. Once they clear his fingerprints, he will be released."

"Yes, thank God!" I smiled.

"Now the only thing is, they said this scan will take forty-five days. During that time, Julius will have to stay in jail." He shook his head.

"What! Why?" I yelled and Rashad rubbed my back again.

"They're unfortunately taking their time with this one sweetie. But that's the lowest I got them to go, they told me ninety days at first. Now it's forty-five or less, and I promise that I will stay on their asses!" Benjamin assured me.

I couldn't do anything but break down and cry, for what seemed like hours.

Benjamin told me I could visit Julius in one week, and that broke my heart. I missed him so much already. I cried the whole drive home, even when dropping Rashad off. Once I got home, I grabbed my chunky baby Jackson, and put him in the bed with me. I played with him for a little bit, and it helped stop the constant tears. I didn't know how long I could be without Julius. It was starting to feel like old times again.

3 DAYS LATER

I was lying on the plush couch that was connected to an ottoman, with my feet stretched out. I was with Jackson and Winnie, watching a show called *Devious Maids* on Hulu. I'd never seen this show before, but it was really interesting.

My phone was being blown up between Menzo, Lucy, Paula, and Rashad checking on me. I was replying to everyone except Lucy and Menzo, because they were on my shit list. My phone rang again, and it was unknown.

"Hello?"

"You have a collect call from Charleston County Detention Center, do you accept the charges?"

"Yes!" I yelled and ran upstairs to the bedroom. "Julius?"

"Hey baby," he replied.

"Are you okay?" I asked.

"I've had better days, but how are you and Jackson?" he replied.

"We're fine, but we miss you."

"I miss you too, and your soft ass skin. I can't wait to feel you again," he said.

"Me either, daddy. I will be there to see you in four days," I smiled, as if he could see me.

"You been counting down?" he asked.

"Yes. Are they being mean to you in there?"

"Nah, everybody is cool. I built relationships with the right people, so I'm living comfy right now. I just miss you and my son already. Fuck," he exhaled.

"I love you Julius Christian Tate." I smiled.

"I love you too Natalia Lillian Tate," he replied, making me blush. "Well goodnight baby girl. It was nice hearing your voice."

"Yours too," I said as tears ran down my face.

"Keep it tight for daddy."

"Of course," I replied and then we hung up.

I cried for a couple minutes more, and then returned to the living room to finish watching TV. I admit I did feel a little better after speaking to him.

JULIUS

1 WEEK LATER

I couldn't wait to get out of this place. By the grace of God, I built relationships with the right people, so I had my own little cell. This nasty ass food and being confined in this musty ass box, was not doing it for me, however. I missed my freedom already, and being laid up with my beautiful woman.

Today my brother was coming to see me, just to update me on a couple things. I couldn't wait to see him and discuss what was going on with the operation. I also got good news from Benjamin. He said that the forty-five days, was now only thirty, and that it may drop even more.

"Tate! You got a visitor," the guard yelled, as he pulled back the cell gate.

I was escorted out into the visiting room, and I spotted my brother immediately. I was thankful that my brother didn't look stressed. He always showed his emotions on his face, and if he looked worried that meant something was wrong.

"What's up player?" I smiled and he stood up to dap me up. The guards glared at us, but we were sitting down by the time they thought to say anything.

"So how are you?" Rashad asked.

"I'm not in my usual element," I replied and he laughed. "So how is umm, business?" I asked.

"The club is doing great as usual. Everything is working smoothly like always," he winked and I nodded.

"That's good to hear man. I was worried for a second. I didn't want to lose everything I worked for," I smiled and nodded.

"But uh Julius, I wanted to talk to you about Menzo man."

"What about him?"

"When I was putting Benjamin's number in Natalia's phone, Menzo started texting her. And from what I could see, he tryna fuck with Natalia," he said.

My heartbeat sped up, and my mouth started to get dry at just thought of he and Natalia fucking around; especially while I was behind bars, and not able to do anything.

"What did you see?" I asked, not sure if I wanted to know.

"He was saying he wanted to see her, another one came in saying he had a dream about her, begging her to let him eat her pussy, and then how he could treat her better than you. All the shit he shouldn't be texting her," he shook his head.

I swallowed the lump in my throat and my stomach started to hurt. This nigga had me beyond fucked up, and I was starting to think he was the one who set me up.

"What does she say?"

"Stop texting me, or leave me alone. Shit like that," he replied.

"I think that nigga set me up," I glared at the wall.

"Well, once the fingerprints come back, we will know who it was."

"And I can't wait," I replied shaking my head.

I chopped it up with my brother for a little longer, and then went back to my cell. I couldn't stop thinking about what he told me about Menzo. I was happy to hear that Natalia was denying his advances, but how long could that last? When she visited tomorrow, I would talk to her about it.

THE NEXT DAY

"Tate!" the guard yelled to let me know I had a visitor.

I walked out as fast as I could, 'cause I couldn't wait to see my baby girl. I walked into the visiting area and saw her sitting down. She looked just as sexy as ever. She had on a black tube dress, black stilettos, and her long brown hair was hanging down.

"Hey ma," I said creeping up on her.

"Julius," she hopped up, grabbed my face, and kissed me about four times.

"Hey!" the guard yelled.

We pulled away from each other and sat down at the table. She stared at me for a little bit, as tears raced down her smooth caramel cheeks. I would've wiped them, but I didn't feel my hands were clean enough.

"So how is everything?" I asked.

"It's been better," she replied.

"Why? What's wrong?" I asked. *Tell me about this fuck nigga Menzo*, I thought.

"The only thing wrong is that you're not at home," she half smiled.

"So nothing else is happening?" I asked.

"No, everything is pretty much the same. I was thinking of going to school," she smiled.

I couldn't respond right away, because I didn't understand why she wouldn't mention anything about another nigga begging to eat her pussy. Really Natalia? Maybe she wanted this nigga.

"Oh yeah, like Paula?" I finally responded and she nodded. "So you've been telling me everything that's going on when I call?"

"Yeah, life is pretty boring without you. Jackson, Winnie, and I just relax all day, or clean and cook," she chuckled.

"Alright, well I'm gonna go back to my cell." I said standing up.

"Why Julius? We still have time left," she said looking up at me.

"Don't come visit me no more, until you can be honest with me," I spat.

"Be honest with you? What are you talking about Julius? I am being honest!" she started to cry.

"And why you dressed like that? The fuck you going later?" I growled.

"I wore this for you Julius," she replied in a low tone.

"I'm ready to go back," I said to the guard and he nodded.

"Julius!" Natalia yelled out to me. "Julius!" she yelled again, using all the strength in her petite frame.

That should teach her lying ass a lesson. Why the fuck wouldn't she want me to know that a nigga I'm supposed to be cool with, is texting her sexual shit? What if Rashad hadn't found out, I would be in the dark. That's probably what she wanted, so she could have some side dick while I'm locked up. But she got shit twisted if she thinks she gone be hopping off Menzo's dick, and then coming to see me.

I was still in shock because of the way Julius treated me. I thought everything was going good, but I guess I was wrong. I kept replaying our conversation over in my head, trying to figure out what went wrong. Maybe he didn't want me going to school.

I went back the next day to visit him, but they let me know that I was no longer on his visiting list. I had them check multiple times, and they confirmed that I'd been removed. I went back to the car, and cried for what seemed like ten minutes, before finally heading back home.

It was around 8pm, and Paula invited Lucy and I to go out. I really didn't want to, but then again, I needed something to keep my mind off of Julius. It was a 21 and over lounge/club, which Lucy and I weren't old enough to get into, but Paula was 21 and the bouncer was her first cousin. She said drinks would be free for us all night, and that is exactly what I needed. Although Lucy couldn't drink, she still wanted to get out and away from Menzo's crazy, creepy ass.

I decided to wear a multicolor, Jeremy Scott patchwork dress that Julius had recently bought me. I wore some Pierre Hardy suede sandal stilettos in pink, and then put my long brown hair in a big bun on top of my head. I threw on some gold studs that I got from H&M, and I was ready.

My phone started to ring, and I prayed it was an unknown number. I walked over and saw that it was.

"Hello?" I answered.

"You have a collect"

"I accept the charges!" I cut the voice off. "Julius?" I smiled.

"What's up?"

"Why did you take me off your visiting list?"

"Cause I don't want to see you," he replied and exhaled heavily.

"Oh, is it cause of school? Because-"

"What you doing?" he asked.

"I'm about to go to a lounge, with Paula and Lucy."

"So you going out and shit, while your nigga is locked up? You couldn't even wait two weeks before you started spreading your legs for another nigga and being a fucking hoe!" he yelled with so much anger in his voice that it made me jump.

"Julius, I'm not doing anything with anybody," I whined. "I don't have to go, I can stay home if you want," I added.

"Nah, you good. Peace."

Click.

As soon as he hung up, my eyes started to water. My phone rang again, but this time it was Paula.

"Hello?"

"I'm outside chica! Hurry up so we can go get Lucy!' she yelled excitedly.

"Okay, I'm coming down now."

I put on some light pink lipstick, and then went to say bye to Winnie and Jackson. I grabbed my jacket from by the door, and then headed out to Paula's car.

"Oohh, you look sexy!" she smiled.

"Thank you," I chuckled.

"What's wrong?" she asked as she started to drive.

"Julius is mad at me."

"Why?" she frowned.

"I really don't know. And when I told him I was going out, he blew up and hung up on me."

"He's just frustrated that he is away from you. He'll be straight once he gets out, watch," she nodded like she was sure.

"Yeah," was all I said, as we continued to Lucy's.

We got to Raye's Lounge, and thankfully Paula's cousin came through. It had a small dance floor for those who just had to dance, but all in all it was a relaxing setting. There were sectioned off couch areas for VIP, which we were thankfully able to sit in. As promised, the waitresses brought us free drinks over, and plenty of extra juice for Lucy.

YG was playing over the lounge, and Paula stood up to shake her ass. Paula was what you called thick; nice big boobs, small waist, big butt, and thick thighs and hips. She wore a tight dress that hugged all her curves. My dress was only tight around the breast area, and since they were small, it was nothing to jump up about. I wasn't tripping though, because my small, round, plump ass matched my B-cups perfectly.

"Come on!" Paula smiled pulling my hand up.

I stood up as well as Lucy, and we all started to dance while drinking. I was happy I came out, because I was having a good ass time. While we were turning up, I saw a group of guys approaching. They looked fresh as hell and all of them appeared to be attractive.

"Hello ladies," the one in front said, staring at me.

"Hi," we all said in unison.

"Do you mind if we come in for a little bit? Or can y'all come to our booth?" he asked as one his friends eyed Paula.

"Uh" I started.

"Y'all can come up here, but bring your bottles," Paula spat, and smiled at the one staring at her.

One of their homies jogged back over to their booth, snatched up their bottles, then came back. We started pouring more drinks, and getting fucked up. I saw one guy talking to Lucy, and I was happy to see that. Even though she was pregnant, she could still pull.

"I don't even know your name beautiful," the guy who was in front of his homies asked.

"Natalia," I nodded.

"Sexy name for a sexy girl. I'm Marlon," he smiled and licked his sexy lips.

Marlon was real cute. He was light skinned with a low fade, and smelled good as hell. He wore a thermal top, jeans, some Nikes and a snapback.

"Nice to meet you Marlon," I smiled.

"So are you seeing anybody? Or..."

"Yeah, I have a boyfriend," I smiled.

"Damn, I'm not surprised ma. Well can we be friends?" he asked.

"Friends?"

"Yeah, like homies," he smiled.

"Okay," I replied.

He handed me his phone, and I typed my number in it. I saw a flash in my face, but I was so twisted that I didn't really care what it was from.

"Thank you. Let me know if that nigga slip up," he bit his lip.

For the rest of the night, we partied with the guys. We drank and danced so hard, that I was sweating by the time I left. The cool air from outside of the club, felt like an air conditioner.

"Let's go to the IHOP on Centre Point, it's open twenty-four hours," Lucy suggested, rubbing her stomach.

"Okay," I slurred. "Let's take a taxi Paula, you're too fucked up," I laughed.

"I can drive Nat," Lucy laughed.

"Oh yeah," I said and we all chuckled. I had forgotten that she didn't drink tonight.

My phone chimed, and I saw I had a text from an unknown number.

(317) 555-5555: Hey beautiful.

Me: Who is thisssss?

(317) 555-5555: Lol. It's Marlon.

Me: Why do you have an Indianapolis area code?

(317) 555-5555: My mom is from out there and we share a plan. She wanted me to pay the bill.

Me: *Oh, I'm from Indianapolis! Lol*

(317) 555-5555: *Yeah? Why you got a Charleston area code then? Lol*

Me: My boyfriend had my number changed a couple months ago.

(317) 555-5555: I see, what you about to do?

Me: Headed to IHOP on Centre Point.

I went ahead and stored his number, before I forgot.

Marlon: *Fasho.*

I locked my phone and rested my head on the headrest. The first thought to enter my mind was Julius. I was happy that he would be home in two and a half weeks, but then again he was angry with me. I shook the thoughts from my head, as we approached IHOP.

When we walked in, I saw Marlon and his homeboys chilling at a table. He looked super good, but I didn't know if it was because I was drunk, or if he was just really cute. He smiled at me and waved me over.

"Let's go sit with them," Lucy said as she led the way.

We walked over and sat down with the men. One of the dudes tried to rub on Paula's thigh, but she stopped them. Marlon draped his arm around me, which seemed innocent to me until I looked at Lucy, and she shook her head at me. I quickly moved Marlon's arm, and cleared my throat.

"My bad, I forgot you had a man," he chuckled and so did his friends.

I remembered that I didn't have any money, so I opened my online banking app before ordering. I smiled when I saw Julius had deposited $20,000 in it for me. I loved his crazy ass so much. That was just spending money, and then he would buy me things on top of that.

"Damn ma!" Marlon said looking at my screen.

"Don't look at my stuff," I frowned and locked my phone. That irritated me that he was all in my business like that.

I scooted away from him a little bit, and stayed that far for the rest of the meal. Once we were all ready to leave, he reached out to give me a hug, but I just walked away from him. I felt guilty and he was kind of annoying.

"Damn, well bye Ms. Natalia!" he called after me.

I didn't even respond, as I headed to the car with my friends. I couldn't wait to just crawl in bed, and cuddle with my son.

Julius would be home in a week and a half, and I was overjoyed. Although he was mad at me, I would set up a nice night for he and I, and he would have no choice but to forgive me. I smiled in the shower, as I rinsed the soap off of my body. Once I was done, I stepped out to brush my teeth and rinse with mouthwash.

"Ah!" I screamed when I saw Menzo sitting in my bedroom, on the lounge chair.

"Good morning beautiful," he smiled.

"Menzo, what are you doing here? Who let you in?" I frowned tightening my towel.

"I let myself in," he smiled.

I looked over and saw Jackson asleep in his little swing. I wanted to call for Winnie, but she took some of my clothes to the dry cleaners, and went to pick up some stuff for my surprise for Julius.

"Wha-what do you want?" I stuttered.

"I just want to watch you get dressed."

"What?"

"I want you to proceed with your normal dressing routine, right here in front of me," he pointed down to the floor.

"I'm not doing anything with"

"You will, or I will make sure these photos of you in the club with some nigga make it to Julius."

I walked over, snatched the four pictures, and wanted to throw up at the sight of me laughing and dancing all on Marlon. *That was where the flash came from*, I thought.

"And don't try to rip them up, because I made about 100 copies," he laughed.

"You just want to watch me?" I asked to make sure.

"Yep," he replied.

"Okay," I nodded.

I walked back by my bed and removed my towel. His eyes roamed my naked body, and he licked his dry lips. His eyes were wide open as he stared. He then pulled his dick out and started to stroke it slowly.

"Do a spin," he said.

I paused for a second and turned around slowly. I then went into my drawer to pull out my underwear and bra. I started to step into my underwear, but he stopped me.

"Lie down on the bed and put your panties on," he demanded.

I took a deep breath, as tears started to escape my eyes. I lay down, and started to slide up my panties. His eyes locked onto my bare vagina, and he started to stroke his dick at a faster pace. I stood back up, and then put on my bra. Usually I would lotion, but I decided to skip that part.

"Stupid ass tatt," he moaned, referring to my tattoo of Julius' name on my rib cage.

I pulled my tube dress over my head, and then shrugged my shoulders to say I was done. By this time, his eyes were closed, and he was nutting all over his hand. He grunted loudly, and then started to pant.

"Fuck. You so damn sexy," he whispered.

He cleaned his hand and dick off with the bottom of his wife beater, like the nasty nigga he was, and then zipped his pants up. He smirked at me and then opened the bedroom door to leave. I immediately grabbed some disinfectant wipes to clean off the doorknobs around the house. I wasn't sure what he touched exactly.

My phone started to ring and I just knew it was Julius. I ran to it, only to see Marlon's name on the screen. He and I had been texting a lot, and since Julius didn't call anymore, we talked until the wee hours of the morning.

"Hello?" I answered.

"What you doing? Let's go have lunch."

"I can't Marlon. I told you I have a boyfriend," I replied.

"I'm starting not to believe you, where is he when I'm talking to you all night?" he chuckled.

"He's busy!"

"Well he seems to be too busy for you. Let me take you out; as busy as he is, he won't even know!" he laughed.

"No! I told you no," I yelled and hung up.

If Menzo hadn't have shown me those pictures this morning, I may have went. But I couldn't chance Menzo being around and taking more footage. It's no telling what he would want from me next.

JULIUS

RELEASE DAY

Ya boy was getting out three days early, and I was fucking ecstatic. I asked my lawyer whose prints were on the drug packaging, and he said they wouldn't give him that info. They said they felt I would try to harm whoever it was, so all they could do is confirm that it wasn't mine. I would find out who it was sooner or later though.

Yesterday I got some pictures in the mail, of Natalia and some nigga chilling and shit in the club. I knew I couldn't trust her little ass. Shit, I would have Jackson tested if he didn't look identical to me. I didn't bother letting her know I was out early either, fuck her. I was just gone go home, grab some shit, and then bounce.

"Hey boo," Franceska smiled once I got in the car.

I was gone have my brother pick me up, but he had to handle some shit. Franceska was the last person I wanted picking me up, but she was the only one available since I wasn't fucking with Natalia.

"Take me by my crib so I can grab some clothes," I said. She smiled and then headed towards my house.

My head was throbbing thinking about all the shit that had transpired during that little ass time I was in jail. I really trusted Natalia, and was really beating myself up for how I treated her hoe ass in the past. Now I felt dumb as hell for trying to make her my fucking wife. Knowing her, she probably fucked Menzo *and* that nigga from the club.

Franceska pulled up to my crib and tried to get out with me, until I told her ass that she could go home. I had my car here, and could drive myself to the hotel I was gone stay in. I got out and ran up my walkway. Once I came in the house, I saw Natalia sitting on the huge ottoman, playing with Jackson. She was wearing her signature tube top and shorts combo, and my dick got hard immediately.

"Julius," Natalia said, as she stood up and walked over to me with Jackson on her hip.

"Hey little man," I said ignoring her and kissing his cheek.

I walked past her and up the stairs to our room, so that I could pack my clothes. As soon as I got in the bedroom, Natalia came in and closed the door.

"Why didn't you tell me you were getting out?" she asked. I didn't say anything, as I took some boxers out the drawer. "Where are you going?" she said touching my forearm.

I snatched my arm away and slapped her across the face. Her nose busted and started dripping blood. She grabbed her nose, and I pushed her to the floor.

"Julius! Stop!' she screamed as I picked her back up by her hair.

"You fucking hoe ass bitch! I'm locked up and you out here fucking some random nigga! I ain't even been gone that damn long!" I yelled as I shook her body by her hair.

I pushed her away and then slapped her as hard as I could. She fell on the bed, and I climbed on top of her. I pulled her head back by her hair, and bit down on her shoulder. I was so mad, that I was just trying to think of any way to inflict pain on her.

"Ahhhhhh! Julius stop! I haven't bee-Ah!" she was cut off when I slapped her ass again.

"What the fuck did I tell you? I told you not to open your hoe ass legs for no other nigga!" I said through gritted teeth in her ear. I wrapped my hands around her neck and Winnie came busting in.

"Please Mr. Tate! You're going to kill her!" Winnie yelled.

I let her go, and stormed out as Natalia cried like a newborn baby. I guess she wanted more, because her slutty ass came running down the stairs after me.

"Julius! I didn't do anything!" she yelled after me.

I realized I forgot my keys in the house, but spotted Franceska's annoying ass still waiting outside for me. I jogged to her car, with Natalia hot on my heels. As soon as I slid in, Natalia punched the window, and it shattered in my lap. Franceska screamed loud as hell, as I hopped out and threw Natalia's ass over my shoulder. I went back in the house, and threw her on the bed. I pinned her hands down and stared down into her beat up face. *Why the fuck did I still love her? She was a whore.*

"Stay yo' ass in here!" I yelled in her face.

"No! You're mine! I don't want you with that bitch!" she cried and locked her legs around my waist.

I couldn't help myself. I pressed my lips against her bloody ones, and dipped my tongue in her mouth. I let her hands go, and she wrapped them around my neck. I wrapped my arms around her small frame, as we got lost in our passionate kiss.

"I promise I haven't been with anyone but you Julius," she whispered in between kisses. I removed her shorts and panties together, as I kissed her flat stomach. "We were just at the club together that's it," she added as I made my way down to her pussy.

I inhaled the sweet smell of it, before planting kisses along the slit. I pulled her clit into my mouth, and stuck two fingers into her pussy. I sucked her clit and plunged my fingers inside her, until she came three times. The smell and taste was just as good as it was before I left. I stood up and undressed, then went to get a warm towel out of our bedroom bathroom. I quickly but gently, cleaned Natalia's face up, and then dipped my tongue in her mouth. I lifted her legs over my arms, and forced my way into her super tight walls.

"I see you were telling daddy the truth," I moaned as I stroked her tight wet walls.

She moved her legs off my arms, and pulled me towards her. She sucked on my lips, as I continued to thrust into her.

"I'll always be honest daddy, I love you," she said in between kisses.

I pulled her tube top down to her belly button, and started to suck on her hard nipples. I kissed back up to her soft lips, and then sped up my pace.

"Ahhh," she moaned as she gushed onto my rod.

"Fuck, I'm about to cum Nat," I groaned into her mouth. I knew Winnie thought we were some fucking psychopaths. One minute we're fighting, and the next we're fucking.

She pushed me back out of her, and then took my dick into her mouth. She went full speed ahead, sucking me up until I busted down her throat. She licked me clean, and then I went to run us a bubble bath.

"I'm sorry I hit you," I said as she straddled my lap in the tub.

"I know," she said looking away.

"I'm gone do better aight," I replied turning her face to me.

"I know," she half smiled.

"You gonna marry me this weekend?" I smiled kissing her lips.

"Really?" she said looking into my eyes. Her honey golden skin glowed in the dimly lit bathroom.

"Yeah, really," I chuckled.

She smiled big and then blushed. She covered her face with both hands, out of embarrassment. She was so adorable. I moved her hands out of her face and kissed her lips. She slid down on my dick, and we both moaned in each other's mouths, not breaking our kiss. Fuck, I loved this girl.

"Fuck." I moaned as Menzo thrusted into my walls.

"What's your name, tell me your name sexy," he grunted. I rolled my eyes, 'cause I was tired of this shit.

"I'm Natalia daddy," I cooed.

"Arrgghhh!" he yelled as he nutted.

Yeah, this was a new thing for Menzo and me. I had to turn off the lights, and pretend I was my best friend, in order to bring my man to an orgasm. That was the story of my sex life. I decided that after the baby was born, I was moving out. I couldn't do this shit with him anymore.

"That was the fucking best," he said out of breath, as we laid next to each other in the dark.

"Ah!" I yelped as my water broke. "Turn on the light Menzo!" I yelled. I guess I needed the light to make sure.

He cut the light on, and we verified my water had broken. He helped me up and to the car, and then we sped to the hospital.

After ten hours, I welcomed my son Lumar Menzo Ouistin. I refused to name him Menzo Jr, when he may never see him again. I knew Menzo had no plans of fathering him. I went ahead and gave him the nigga's name as a middle name, just out of the goodness of my heart. His trifling ass didn't give a fuck what I named him anyway. He didn't even stay for the delivery.

I'd been home for two days, and I was ready to get as far away from Menzo as possible. I hated him so much, and I was happy that the healing time was weeks away from being over. I was happy to have a reason not to fuck his whack ass. Plus, I knew he had some little bitch he was fucking on the side, and that was cool with me.

Today, Natalia and I were gonna secretly look at apartments. She was gonna use part of the money that Julius gave her, to help me pay my rent and the deposit. Here she was paying my way, like she'd been doing ever since I met her.

"Now this is one of our best condominiums, it's two stories..." the realtor started.

I stopped listening after a while, because I really didn't care about what she was saying. I just needed Natalia to pay her the money, so we could hit up the furniture store. I nodded as if I was paying attention, and they both looked at me waiting for my approval.

"I like it. I will take it!" I said.

"Well how much is it?" Natalia asked. "Monthly," she continued.

"Natalia! Why does it matter?" I scowled.

"Lucy, I just want to know," she replied and I rolled my eyes.

"$1500 a month," the realtor smiled.

"Okay that's fine," Natalia replied.

After signing all the paperwork, and paying the first and last month's rent, we headed to Pottery Barn to buy some furniture. We both got stuff for our son's, and then I got stuff for my new place. She spent about $10,000 on me in total, and boy was I happy.

Once we knew everything was placed in my condo, she dropped me off at my new place, after taking me grocery shopping. I swear Natalia was like my sugar daddy. I appreciated it though.

Lumar was knocked out, so I laid him down on my new couch,

and then poured me a glass of the wine I stole from Menzo's crib. I pulled out my phone, and shot Julius a text. When Natalia went to the bathroom earlier, I took Julius number out her phone. Yeah, I'm shady or whatever, but I really don't care. You see how you feel after your nigga asks you to pretend to be your best friend in bed.

Me: Hey sexy.

2 HOURS LATER

Julius: Who is this?

NATALIA

JULY 25TH

"Introducing, Mr. and Mrs. Julius Christian Tate!" the DJ yelled over the reception hall, and every one clapped.

Julius leaned down to kiss my lips about one hundred times, before we walked into the reception hall. We headed to the middle of the dance floor to have our first dance, and it was one of the greatest moments in my life. I never thought I would see this day, where Julius and I would be married. I never even thought I would be married period. We wanted to dance to "All Eyes on You" by Meek, since that was our song, but we went ahead with our second favorite, "Red Eye" by Amerie, since it was more appropriate. Right after however, the DJ played Meek for us.

I was happy that my mother decided to come. I think she only came because Julius paid for her to be here, but I was still happy to see her nonetheless. We went ahead and sat down at the table designated for us, and I had Paula and Lucy sitting at the left of me. My baby, Jackson sat in his daddy's lap, as we ate food and cake. Lucy was really quiet the whole time, but I wasn't gonna let her attitude ruin this day for me. Paula was being a great friend as usual, so I was mainly talking to her. I didn't have time to coddle Lucy.

"I just want to say a couple words to my little bro and his beautiful wife." Rashad stood up and put his glass in the air. Everyone quieted down and looked his way. "I thought I would never see the day where you'd be a married man, especially before me. But I'm happy for you dawg, and I couldn't have picked a better sister-in-law," Rashad smiled, and everyone clapped except Lucy. I rolled my eyes and Paula shook her head.

We had a really good time all night, and I was beat. I wanted to get some sleep, but we had to head to Paris overnight, so I would just sleep on the plane. Paula and Rashad were coming too, and I wanted Lucy there, but Julius said that wasn't a good idea. And with the way she was acting all day at my wedding, I was definitely agreeing with his decision now.

<hr>

We got to Paris early in the morning, and after getting dressed for the day, we headed to Disneyland in Paris. I'd never been to Disneyland or Paris so my mouth seemed to be stuck open the whole time.

"I don't know what this is, but let's go!" I smiled as I pointed to the Sleeping Beauty Castle attraction. Julius shook his head and smiled.

"Aye, come here," he said pulling me back into him. "You been so excited, I haven't gotten any lip action," he smiled. I chuckled as he pressed his lips against mine, and then sucked my lips.

"Aight y'all!" Rashad yelled.

I took about a million pictures during the whole time we were there. My Instagram was flooded with pictures of Pocahontas' Indian Village, the Pinocchio attraction, Ratatouille, and us meeting Mickey Mouse. I had millions of pictures of the four of us, and then some of my love and I. I had so many souvenirs it was crazy. I hadn't been sad one time, and we'd only been here a day.

We left the park, and headed to our suite at Le Bristol Paris. We had to get ready to go to dinner within the hotel. It was being hosted by one of the greatest chefs in town, so they say, and we were gonna have a great meal. I hoped he was really good, because I had never tasted French food before.

We went our separate ways, and Julius and I walked into our suite. I loved this suite much more than the one in Los Angeles. It reminded me of those French romance films. The living room was huge, with white couches and burgundy lounge chairs. There were two bedrooms, even though we only needed the master bedroom. The master bedroom was huge and had bay windows that gave a view over all of Paris it seemed. There were pure white relaxing chairs and French pictures on the wall. It was gorgeous, and I knew it cost my man, excuse me, my husband a lot of money. The bathrooms were all white, and they had plush robes in them. There was a balcony connected to the bathroom, so that we could take a bubble bath while watching the stars.

KNOCK!

KNOCK!

KNOCK!

A young man came to the door to deliver a complimentary bottle of French champagne. We were in the honeymoon suite, so I guess they did that for all newlyweds. I wasn't 21 yet, but I don't think they cared in Paris. Plus, Julius was 21 anyway.

"I love this honey," I smiled, as I took the glass of champagne he poured me.

"Honey?" he chuckled.

"Yes, honey. That's what married couples say." I chuckled as he towered over me to kiss my lips.

"Is that right Mrs. Tate?" he asked, as I smiled and stared up into his eyes for a couple seconds. I silently prayed that I didn't ever wake up, if this was actually a dream.

"I am Mrs. Tate hunh?" I grinned.

"You are. The one and only," Julius replied before kissing me.

It was only 7pm, so we decided to take a bubble bath together, since we had two hours to get down to the ballroom for dinner. I pinned my curly hair up, and slid into the huge tub with my man. I sat between his legs, as we sipped champagne, and stared out the balcony doors.

"Ahhh, I love you," I said leaning my head back on his chest.

"I love you more baby girl," he replied kissing my cheeks.

I was all dressed up for dinner, in my favorite designer Jeremy Scott. I wore a knit striped crop top, with the matching skirt. The crop top was short sleeved, and a mixture of red and orange-yellow stripes. The skirt was the same, and stopped in the middle of my thigh. I finished it off with some patchwork stilettoes from Tom Ford. I pinned my long, brown curls up loosely, and let them fall where they may. Julius wore an all-black Givenchy suit. All black meaning the shirt, jacket, pants and shoes were black. He wore a tie that was black, with little white specs on it. His hair was freshly cut since the wedding day, and his Dolce cologne was just as intoxicating as the first time I smelled it.

"You look so good Nat. Damn," Julius said looking me up and down.

He put his hand out to lead me to the ballroom. We met up with Paula and Rashad, before being seated. The chef was really nice, and everything was so upscale. Rashad and Julius were being so mushy, and Paula and I loved every bit of it. I posted plenty of pictures of Julius and I, and Paula and I, and I guess Lucy wasn't feeling it.

Lucy Bff: Wow you knew I needed to get away, so much for a best friend.

I felt bad, but she was really acting strange, and I just wanted to enjoy my honeymoon. Anyway, I tasted all kinds of wines and champagnes, so I was so damn tipsy. I was full, and ready to have sex with my husband. After a couple hours, we all retired to our suites to prepare for the next day's festivities.

"We're making another baby tonight," Julius smiled as he unbuttoned his shirt.

I was laying on the bed in a peach lace, bra and thong set. I left my hair in the same style from dinner. Julius crawled onto the bed and got between my legs. He kissed my lips, as he pulled down my panties. He reached under me to unsnap my bra, and then devoured my nipples.

"Ahhh, oooh," I purred. I was buzzed so it seemed to intensify everything.

Julius placed my thighs on his shoulders, and sucked my clit into his mouth. He placed his palms under my thighs to push them back, as he used his tongue wisely. He licked from my opening, to my swollen clit, where he would softly suck on it. I thought I was gonna pass out I was cumming so hard on his mouth.

"Ahhh, ahhh. I love you Ju! Ahhh," I cried as I ran my hand over his fade.

My body jerked once more, as I exploded for the third time. He lay on his back, after kissing my thighs, and I took his long thick dick into my mouth. I paid a lot of attention to the head, as I played with his balls. Once my mouth was soaked, I took the rest of him in my mouth.

"Natalia, shit," he mumbled as he grabbed a fistful of my hair.

I bobbed up and down, switching up my speed, and keeping it sloppy just the way he liked it. In no time, he was shooting his seeds down my throat. I swallowed it up, and then climbed atop it. I slid down slowly, and we both bit our lips simultaneously at the feeling.

"This pussy was made for me," Julius moaned.

I rocked my hips slowly, making sure to bounce slowly the way he liked. He grabbed my small perky breasts, and began to play with my nipples. My pelvis tightened, and I squeezed my thighs against his rib cage. I released all over his pole, and he sat up to flick his tongue over my nipples. He flipped me on my back, and then rushed into me. He pinned my hands up, and dipped his tongue in my mouth. We were sucking each other's lips, as he rushed into me and pulled out slowly, constantly. I came two more times, before he finally cuffed my shoulders within his biceps, and pounded into me until he came. He kissed me while still pumping me at an extremely slow pace.

"I love yo' sexy ass," he whispered in between kisses.

"I love you too husband," I replied trying not to break our kiss.

We made love for the rest of the night, and I'm sure I was gonna come back to South Carolina pregnant.

I had the time of my life for the rest of the trip, sightseeing, trying new foods, just getting into the Parisian life. Julius and I decided to get our wedding date tattooed on the napes of our necks, in roman numerals. Luckily since we arrived at the time we did, we got to experience the Paris Plagues, which is like an artificial beach. Paula and I took so many bikini pictures. I really went overboard, because I knew my body wasn't gonna look like this anymore for a while.

JULIUS

I 'd been back from my honeymoon for two weeks now, and I couldn't stop thinking about it. I had never been so relaxed in my life. I felt like a totally new person, and in a way, I guess I was. I was a married man now, and was the official King of South Carolina. My businesses were flourishing, both legal and illegal, and just as I predicted, I had more money than I could count.

Tomorrow afternoon, I would be surprising my wife with our new house. Everything was finished and completely furnished. I couldn't wait to see the look on her face.

"Excuse me," I said to the young lady I bumped into. I was at my Club Rissani just to make sure everything was going good, and to double check my books. "Bianca?" I frowned.

"Hey Ju," she smirked and sipped her drink.

"What you doing in Charleston?" I asked.

"Oh, just visiting some friends," she nodded

"You have friends in Charleston?" I raised a brow.

"Yeah I do. Guess you didn't know me as well as you thought Ju," she licked her lips.

"Aight, well it was nice seeing you," I replied and turned to walk away.

"Wait! So you married now?" she asked lightly touching my arm.

"Yeah, I am," I nodded.

"To Natalia, the girl you told me you wasn't feeling, no matter how many times I asked you," she shook her head.

"Well I guess you knew what was up all along, right?" I shrugged and walked away, before she could respond.

I didn't have time to go back and forth with her. What was the point? Natalia and I were married, and Bianca and I have been over for at least a fucking year. She shouldn't even be worried about me at this point.

Before heading home, I wanted to check on the construction of the winery/restaurant I was building. Bart said I was making way more money than what the club could make, and that I needed another business to make my money look legit. I agreed with him, and decided to open "Jackson Beach Winery". It was a restaurant and winery, with a beach theme. Natalia was the brains behind it, so I made sure to make her a partial owner. I wanted her to have her own money coming in, in case something happened to me.

After checking with Clayton on the progress of the winery, I headed home to my baby. She said she had something to tell me, so I was eager to hear. I bobbed my head to "No Role Modelz" by J.Cole as I drove, and chuckled at a couple of the lines in the song. J.Cole always spoke the truth, and didn't give a damn who it offended, kind of like me. I pulled into my driveway, and then the garage. When I walked into my house, "It's Whatever" by Aaliyah was playing throughout, and there were candles everywhere.

"Natalia?" I called out as I closed the door.

Before I could finish calling her name, she came down stairs in a sexy black lace one-piece. It was cut out on the sides, showing my name tatted on her rib cage. Her long hair was hanging down and swinging, as she walked up to me. She wrapped her arms around my neck, and pulled me down a little, for a kiss.

"What is all this?" I chuckled.

"We're celebrating!" she smiled, and pushed me down onto the couch.

She straddled me and kissed my neck. My hands roamed all over her soft petite frame, and squeezed her little plump ass. I grabbed her body, and began kissing on the exposed parts of her small breast.

"Don't you want to know what we're celebrating?" she chuckled.

"Oh yeah, what?" I smiled.

"Weelllll, we're gonna have a baby," she smiled big as fuck.

I pulled her close and kissed her hard as hell. It was so sexy to know that she was carrying my baby again. I stood up with her still straddling me, and took her upstairs to possibly make that baby a twin.

***

"Aight, when I move my hand, open your eyes," I said to Natalia, while holding Jackson on my hip.

"Okay," she replied smiling.

"Aight, open them," I said.

She opened her eyes, and her jaw dropped. She stared at the big ass house, for what seemed like forever.

"Go look around. It's our new house. We even have a room for Winnie, like you wanted."

"Julius..." she said as she slowly walked towards the house.

Together, the three of us looked around the mansion. I made sure to keep her out as long as I could, so her wardrobe could be moved over before we arrived. Everything looked perfect, and I was gonna make sure that Clayton got a nice little bonus for doing such a good job.

Today, Lucy and I were going over to Paula's house. Her mom was gonna make us lunch, since she wanted to hear about our trip to France. It was such a happy moment for me, so I didn't mind telling it to anyone who would listen. My grandkids are gonna be tired of me talking about it.

Lucy was still acting strange, and she didn't want to talk about my trip to Paris at all. Whenever I brought it up, or showed her a picture, she would always bring up how bad Julius treated me when we first met. She pretty much had it in her head that I was shady for not inviting her. I just gave up on apologizing, and hoped she got over it. I felt bad that I was happy she didn't come. I didn't think about her once, or anything else negative while in Paris, and it felt so good. Our next trip though, I would be sure to bring her.

"So, tell me about this honeymoon," Paula's mom, Sandra smiled, as she sat down some fresh lemonade.

"Oh it was cool," I replied not wanting to say too much.

"Cool? Natalia, tell my mom how much fun we had!" Paula smiled with excitement.

I looked over at Lucy, and she appeared to be occupied with her phone. I decided to go ahead and use this time to my advantage, and tell Sandra everything about my trip.

"Well, when we first got there, we went to Disneyland and I got to see all the Disney princesses, and meet Mickey Mouse. It was so fun, I felt like a kid again," I smiled, as I adjusted Jackson in my lap. "We stayed in this really nice hotel named, Le Bristol, and it was like a mini French apartment. It was really pretty, and I have a gang of pictures if you'd like to see. Oh! And then we had dinner in the"

"Nobody wants to hear you brag about your perfect little life Natalia! Don't forget that Julius beat your ass about five days before the wedding, when he got out of jail!" Lucy cut in to say.

"Oh my gosh!" Sandra said covering her mouth in shock. I was so embarrassed.

"I'm getting real fucking tired of your attitude!" Paula spat.

"I don't give a fuck what you're tired of! Natalia tryna act like her shit is all sunshine and flowers, when we know that ain't the case!" Lucy yelled. "You weren't there when he was cheating and dissing her every other week, I was!" she continued and jammed her finger in her chest.

"Nah, you just a hating ass bitch! That's what it is. And that's exactly why yo' ass wasn't invited to Paris. Instead of being happy for your so called best friend, you pouting like a bitch!" Paula yelled back.

"Ladies!" Sandra yelled, and moved Paula's daughter Gabby out of her lap.

Jackson started to cry, so I hugged him tightly and kissed his cheek. After rocking him a little bit more, he finally calmed down. I straightened his clothes, and then pulled his toy keys out of my purse.

"Now, Natalia, please continue sweetie," Sandra half smiled.

"No, maybe I shou"

"Please, I'd like to hear," Sandra smiled again with pleading eyes.

"Okay. Well we had a nice dinner in this huge beautiful dining room. The food was umm, let's just say it was interesting, but it was good. It seems like they put alcohol in everything," I smiled, and Paula and Sandra laughed.

"We also went to the little mock beach Ma, it was so nice. Natalia and I took a gang of pictures in our little thong bikinis." Paula smiled showing her mom some pictures in her phone. "Nat and Julius were so cute together! I had to sneak and take some candids of them." Paula smiled and I squinted my eyes playfully like I was angry.

"I'm so happy to hear that. Lucy honey, would you like a refill on your lemonade?" Sandra asked, and Lucy shook her head. "Paula also tells me you and your husband, have moved into a new house Nat."

"Yeah, we got a big house. It has five bedrooms, a gym, and all kinds of stuff. My favorite part of the house is the backyard. It's so big, and the grass is beautiful. There is also a patio cover, so we can relax in the back while people swim and stuff." I smiled starting to feel all giddy inside. "We are thinking of having Jackson's first birthday there, so you guys should come then," I nodded and they smiled.

"You know I will be there, I can't wait to see this house Nat," Sandra smiled, and sipped her lemonade.

"Can you take me home Natalia?" Lucy barged in.

"We haven't even eaten yet Lucy," I frowned.

"Well, I lost my appetite listening to your damn fairytale!"

"Oh my gosh! Say one more disrespectful thing to Nat, and I'm slapping you I swear!" Paula said with her eyes closed, like she was trying to calm herself down.

"Ain't my fault she thinks her abusive, cheating ass husband is a pri"

Before she could finish, Paula punched her in the face. Lucy hopped up and tried to get to her, but Sandra held her back. The glasses of lemonade, including the pitcher, all fell over and rolled onto the floor.

"I'm gonna beat yo' ass bitch!" Lucy yelled as she tried to get past Paula's mother.

"Come on weak hoe!" Paula chuckled while waving her hands, signaling Lucy to come closer.

"We are just gonna leave," I said, adjusting Jackson on my hip and grabbing my purse.

I walked out and Lucy followed. She got in and slammed my passenger door, as I buckled Jackson in his car seat. I glared at her, because I was so angry. If Lucy had have been anybody else and not my best friend, I would've punched her stupid ass myself. But because she was my girl, or used to be, I let her dumb ass act out.

"What is your fucking problem Lucy?!" I said as soon as I got into the driver's seat.

"Nothing," she replied.

"Well until you can figure out what it is, I don't want to hang with you anymore," I said pulling off.

"Wooooow. You got a new homegirl and a rock on your finger, so now you too good for Lucy." She nodded slowly.

"No, that ain't the case and you know that!"

"Then what is the case Nat?" she asked turning in her seat to face me.

"You're mean as fuck. All you try to do is bring me down. Anytime I bring up Julius and me, you find some way to bring up all the bad stuff he's done," I replied.

"I'm sorry Natalia," she exhaled heavily, and pinched the bridge of her nose. "I'm just really depressed right now. I have a new baby, and a baby daddy who is in love with my best friend. It makes me hate you, but I'm working on it."

"Don't let Menzo come between us Lucy," I frowned, shaking my head.

"You're right, I'm gone get it together," she said as I pulled up to her condo.

"Okay," I said hitting the unlock button. I was ready for her to get out.

I was tired of Lucy, and I think we needed a break. Maybe a break would give her some time to think and not be so angry. If anybody knows about Julius and my problems in the past, it's me. I really didn't need her bringing it up every chance she got. I sped home as fast as I could, trying to clear my head. I just wanted to get home to my man, so we could cuddle with our baby.

JULIUS

I was having a little meeting with my team, but before I did, I wanted to talk to and fire Menzo's snake ass. Because I was firing him, I didn't want him hearing any details about the operation. Also, if he wanted to get stupid and try to rat me out, he would come up short with information, since I was changing everything around.

"You wanted to see me?" Menzo smiled as he strolled in.

"Yeah, sit," I replied and waited until he did so. "I know about the texts you send, and have sent to Natalia," I started.

"Man, so the fuck what," he shrugged and chuckled.

I had to sit up and take a good look at this muthafucka, because that couldn't have just come out of his mouth.

"So the fuck what? You sending sexual shit to my wife is a muthafucking problem for me, in case you ain't realized that." I squinted my eyes as if the sight before me was hard to see. This couldn't be Menzo getting too big for his draws; he had to have been drunk.

"I realized it, but I didn't care," he raised a brow as to say *yeah nigga I just said that.*

"You think this is a damn game Menzo?" I frowned.

"Hey, you know about that honey she got between her legs. I'm just as addicted as you."

"Are you tryna tell me, you fucked my wife?" I asked feeling my skin get hot.

"I sure am," he smirked.

"Yeah right nigga. Natalia knows better," I scoffed, while making sure my gun was in reach.

"Well, usually she knows better. However, you were in jail, and she was feeling vulnerable. I was a shoulder to lean on. I made sure to kiss every part of her body, especially the little Marilyn Monroe mole she has on her right hip," he said licking his lips.

"Oh you a funny guy I see," I smirked.

I cocked my gun and aimed it at him. His eyes got big, and a bunch of words stammered over themselves, as they left his mouth. I put my silencer on, and pulled the trigger. I shot him in his stomach three times. He started to cough up blood, and I watched him suffer for a little bit.

"Please man, call for help," he begged as blood spilled out of his mouth, and he clutched his stomach.

I smiled and sipped my Hennessey as I watched him suffer. I finally called Dash and Leese in for cleanup, once he succumbed to his injuries. *Bitch ass nigga.* Now it was time to deal with my hoe of a wife.

I sped into my garage, damn near driving through the wall of our new home. I couldn't believe I married her ass, and she had fucked Menzo. How else would he know about something on her body like that? The mole was maybe a little bigger than a piece of pepper, so I knew he saw her naked.

"So you fucked Menzo?" I said to Natalia, as she floated in the pool.

"What? Julius no!" she replied. She climbed out of the pool and I slapped her back in it. Blood started to mix with the pool water, as she submerged under and then shot back up breathing heavily. I stormed into the house, and a few minutes later she was following me.

"You cannot keep hitting me Julius!" she cried as she watched me pace the bedroom.

"You ain't got to worry about me hitting you, 'cause we're getting a damn divorce," I spat and plopped on the bed.

"Why? I never had sex with anybody in the state of South Carolina but you! I've never had sex with anybody in the world but you!" she cried as she closed the bedroom door.

"How the fuck would Menzo know about certain parts of your body, that can only be seen when naked Natalia? Are you telling me he's never seen you naked?"

She stared at me, and then looked away. Blood dripped from her lip, and she put her wrist up to it to stop it. I couldn't believe it; she fucked this nigga.

"Wow Natalia, you really fucked this nigga! Who else you been fucking?" I said standing up, and nearing her with my fists clenched.

"Julius, remember I'm pregnant," she pleaded as she backed away.

"That probably ain't my fucking baby!" I yelled.

"I did not sleep with Menzo, Julius. Yes he saw me naked, but that was it!" she cried.

"Well, I just want you to know, your real baby daddy is dead!" I shouted.

"I told you I never had sex with him! You know this is your baby!" she cried as she pushed me with all her might.

I grabbed her wrists and threw her to the ground. I grabbed as much of her hair as I could, and kneeled down to her face.

"I'll have those divorce papers to you ASAP!" I said through gritted teeth.

As I tried to walk out, she grabbed onto my polo shirt. I turned around and slapped the shit out of her. She flew back and fell to the floor, then sat up with her eyes bucked at me in fear. She brought her trembling hand up to cover her wounds, as I walked out. *Fuck! Why were my feelings so strong for this girl?*

I turned around and walked back into the bedroom. I picked Natalia up bridal style, and took her to the bathroom to clean her up. She was sniffling, and blood was dripping from her face. I was the worst nigga, but then again she shouldn't have slept with Menzo.

"I-I didn't do anyth" she attempted to say, as I dabbed the warm towel on her nose and lips.

"Shhh ma, I don't know what to believe right now. But regardless, I need to leave and clear my head. I can't keep putting my hands on you like this," I replied honestly and she nodded. "I hope you are telling me the truth though, because I love you so fucking much," I added and kissed her soft lips.

"I love you too," she replied in between kisses.

I wrapped my arms around her small frame, and held her tightly. She put her arms around my neck, and we pressed our bodies against each other's as hard as we could. I carried her to the bed, and then laid her down. I placed the covers over her body, and then kissed her lips again. I needed sometime away to think clearly.

"Where you going?" she asked as I headed out of the bedroom.

"I just need some time to think baby. I love you," I replied and left.

***

"**S**hit," I moaned as I rammed my dick into Bianca.

"Fuck Ju, you still got good dick daddy," she moaned as she gushed on my dick.

I sped up, and nutted hard as fuck. I slid out, and pulled the condom off to flush it. Afterwards, I went back out into her hotel room to put my clothes back on so I could jet.

"Aight, I'll talk to you soon," I said to Bianca, as I put on my tennis shoes.

"If you're not busy, maybe you can come back tonight?" she smirked.

"We'll see," I replied and dipped.

NATALIA

2 DAYS LATER

I had finally come home from the hospital after Julius fucked me up. My nose and lips were still swollen and bruised. I missed him so much, even though what he did to me was horrible. I loved him more than anything, and yet shit just seemed to always tear us apart. There was no way in hell I was signing divorce papers, when I didn't even do anything.

Winnie, Jackson, and I decided to go and stay back at the condo. That new house just had bad memories, and we hadn't even had it that long. I cried at the thought of it.

I was looking at the printed pictures of our wedding and honeymoon, when I heard a knock at the door. I wasn't expecting anyone because of how bad my face looked, so I was a bit surprised. Winnie was cooking, so I didn't want to disturb her. I walked over with my blanket draped over my back, and looked through the peephole.

"What Marlon?" I yelled through the door.

"I just wanted to check on you. I haven't talked to you in forever," he said.

I paused and then unlocked the door. Marlon was standing there in a grey sweat suit, and matching Nike's. He looked nice, and he smelled good. I gestured for him to come in, and he smiled.

"What happened to your face?" he asked as we sat down on the couch together.

"It's nothing," I replied and looked away to turn on the TV.

He grabbed my chin, and turned me to look at him. He stared into my eyes, as if he was trying to read me.

"So this why you ain't at the house?" Julius asked.

I pulled my face away from Marlon, and stood up. He laughed and shook his head.

"Aye my nigga, get the fuck up out my crib!" Julius glared at Marlon.

"I'm sorry, who are you?" Marlon asked playing dumb. He knew exactly who Julius was.

"I'm gone be the muthafucka that sends yo' ass to your maker if you don't get the fuck out my shit!" Julius replied pulling his gun from his waist.

"Aight, aight, chill," Marlon said hopping up and leaving.

"Julius I"

He rushed me and pinned my hands down on the couch. He hovered over me, and stared into my eyes, as I lay on the couch.

"Don't ever bring another nigga around my son," he said looking into my eyes.

"I-I-" I stuttered and shook my head, as he tightened his grip on my wrists.

"What you think you finna be dating? Did you fuck him too?" he frowned.

"No Julius, I"

He positioned himself between my legs, and kissed my lips hard. He sucked on my lips, as he pressed his body against mine.

"I love you Julius," I whispered in between kisses.

We wrestled our tongues, and made love with our mouths. It'd only been two days, yet I missed him like crazy. Suddenly, he stopped and got up off of me.

"Fuck!" he yelled rubbing his hands over his fresh fade.

"What Ju"

He stormed out before I could finish. My phone buzzed immediately, and I saw it was a text from Julius.

Husband: *Sign the papers when you get them. What just happened meant nothing.*

I tried to blink away tears, as I read it over and over. I locked my phone up, declining to reply, and then lay back down on the couch. I cried myself to sleep, right there.

I was procrastinating like a muthafucka on getting these divorce papers ordered. I couldn't be with Natalia, knowing she was hoeing around. Hell nah. I promised that no shit like this would ever happen to me, and look. I'm married to a fucking hoe, and the worst part is that I'm still in love with her.

"So I already spoke to Bart about upping our shipment. He said it was straight, and just to give him a couple days," I said to my team, as we sat around the conference table.

"So that means, instead of Monday morning, the pickup will be when?" Tim asked.

"It's gonna be Thursday, but only this once, since we arranged all this kind of last minute. After this time, shipments will resume Natalia, what are you doing here?" I said when I saw her walk through the door.

"I need to talk to you," she smiled closing the door behind her. Ninety percent of the niggas admired her beauty, as she locked her eyes on only me. I knew what they all were thinking, but it'd be pointless for me to try and fight everybody. Natalia couldn't help that she was the prettiest bitch from here to Indianapolis.

"One second," I told my people, and led Natalia to my private office. "Aight speak," I said after closing the door.

"I got the first sonogram," she smiled.

"The what?" I frowned and sat down on my office couch.

"The sonogram... the picture of the baby in my stomach." she replied.

"Why you telling me?" I scoffed, as I reach for the Jack Daniels and a glass, on the table next to me.

"Because it's our baby, and I thought you wanted to know like you did last time," she said, playing with the picture in her hands.

I sipped my drink, and looked at her through my glass. She was wearing a yellow halter dress that hugged her small frame. Her small, perky breasts were sitting up perfectly as usual. Her long, brown hair was in a side braid, with curls hanging out the bottom of the ponytail holder. She was glowing, which made her honey golden skin look lickable. I did not want to love her anymore, but I did, with every fiber of my being.

"I don't know whose baby that is," I finally replied and took another sip.

She sat her purse on my desk, and walked over to me. She took my drink out my hand, and sat it back on the end table next to me. She then sat in my lap, and cupped my face before pressing her soft lips against mine. She started to suck my lips, and then dipped her tongue in my mouth. I rubbed all over her small back, as we kissed and kissed.

"You know this is your baby," she whispered in between kisses.

After a couple minutes of hot and heavy tongue action, I finally snapped out of the trance she had over me. I lightly pushed her off of me and on to the couch. I stood up and pinched the bridge of my nose, because I had a headache from all this shit. I hiked my jeans up, as I walked around the back of my desk to sit down and think. I threw my hood on and interlocked my fingers under my chin.

"Julius, I didn't do anything. You need to know that," she said.

"Explain why that nigga knew what your naked body looked like Natalia?" I said looking up at her.

"He blackmailed me," she said as her eyes became watery.

"What?" I frowned in irritation. *What the fuck was she talking about?*

"He took those pictures of me in the club, and he said if I didn't undress in front of him, he would show them to you."

"And you did it?" I replied shaking my head. "And you expect me to believe you didn't let him fuck too?"

"I didn't Julius! That was all he wanted!"

"Oh, so if he wanted some pussy too, you would've done it?" I yelled standing up.

"No! I"

"Just get out Natalia, I have to finish my meeting and I can't deal with this," I said as I walked to my office door, and opened it for her.

She grabbed her purse off my desk, and pushed me as she walked by. I grabbed her arm, and pulled her back to me. I wrapped my arm around her small torso, and leaned down to kiss her lips. She tried to pull away, but my grip was too strong. I kissed from her lips, to her neck, to her collarbone, and then back to suck on her lips. I pecked her once more, and then we stared into each other's eyes. She moved from my embrace and left, after realizing my mind was still made up; Natalia and I were a wrap. No grown man is gone just ask to watch you undress or dress, and then not fuck.

NATALIA

2 WEEKS LATER

I had yet to receive any divorce papers, so I wasn't sure what was going on in Julius' mind. He seemed to be adamant about getting a divorce, and we hadn't seen each other in two weeks. However, today he was coming to the house to see Jackson.

Yes, the house. I decided I was gonna live here, when I heard he was pretty much back with Bianca. She was telling everyone who would listen, that she and Julius were fucking around again. I cried every night damn near, just thinking about him going back to her.

Julius was back to his old ways, smashing everything with two legs, saying our baby wasn't his, and ignoring me for weeks at a time. I should've known our little fairytale life wouldn't last long. Only good thing that seemed to come out of our relationship was Jackson, and that week we spent in Paris.

I threw on some skinny jeans, a t-shirt, and some fuzzy socks. Paula was gonna come over later so that we could relax, and she could see the new house finally. I braided my curly hair into one big braid, and right when I finished, I heard the front door open. I went to Jackson's room, and grabbed him to take him downstairs.

"Mr. Tate is here, Mrs. Tate," Winnie said poking her head into my son's bedroom.

"Okay," I replied and half smiled.

I dressed Jackson in a red polo, and some khaki shorts. He was identical to his father, with his small nose, and beautiful peanut butter complexion. I kissed his little cheeks, and then picked him up to take him downstairs. I walked down the stairs with him on my hip, and Julius stared at us as we neared him.

"Hey man," he smiled as I handed Jackson to him. I turned to walk away, because I wanted to make some lunch and do laundry to help out Winnie. "Where you going?' Julius called after me.

"I'm going to make some lunch," I replied.

"You can't spend no time with your family?" he frowned.

"My family? I didn't know you and I were family Julius. I thought we were getting a divorce, since I'm carrying your friend's baby, right?" I folded my arms.

He placed Jackson in his swing bed and marched over to me. He had on a simple black t-shirt, with dark jeans, and all black chucks. Even the simple things made him look sexy.

"So you finally admitted it," he cracked an evil smile as he towered over me.

"Whatever Julius. If you want to believe this one isn't yours, go ahead. I'm tired of going back and forth with you. I will take care of my baby alone," I said trying to walk away.

"Come here," he said trying to kiss me, but I moved my face away.

"I don't want you kissing me. You think I don't know about you and Bianca?" I frowned.

"Bianca ain't no fucking body! She ain't never been shit to me!" he yelled.

"Well it doesn't seem that way. And she ain't the only one you fucking," I said calmly, as I started to feel tears well up.

"So! You fucked Menzo!" he boomed.

"Well since you think I fucked someone else, then I will just go ahead and do it!" I cried.

He grabbed me by the neck, and pinned me up against the wall. I clawed at his hands, so that I could catch my breath.

"That's what you gone do? Huh, you little hoe!" he said frowning his face up.

I felt bold, so I nodded my head yes. His eyes bucked, and he let go of my neck to slap me. His hand landed on my eye, and it started to throb. I ran away towards the stairs, but he grabbed me by the waist, making us fall on the stairs.

"Stop Julius! I'm pregnant! Just send the divorce papers!" I cried and ran up the stairs. Once I reached the bedroom, I locked the door. He had Winnie bring me some ice for my eye, and I fell asleep after applying it for a little while.

I woke up to my door opening, and saw Julius walking in. I looked at the clock, and saw it was around 6pm. I had been sleep for four hours straight. He was holding a bouquet of white roses, and a gift bag. As he neared me, I turned my face away from him. He set the stuff down on the nightstand next to me, and then sat on the bed. We stared at each other, before I started to cry. He lightly thumbed my tears away, and kissed my bruised eye gently.

"You're gonna kill me Julius," I said slightly above a whisper. "Me and the baby, if you keep hitting me and stressing me out," I cried.

He didn't respond, as he kissed all over my face. He undressed down to his boxers, and then did the same to me. He climbed in bed, and hugged me tight from behind. He kissed my shoulders, and then craned his neck around to kiss my lips. I slightly moved away, as he sucked on my bottom lip. He rubbed his hand down the front of my body, and cupped my still flat stomach. He kissed the tattoo of our wedding date, as he slipped his hand down into my panties.

"I'm sorry I hit you baby," he whispered once he felt me tense up.

I didn't say anything, as he brought his hand around the back of me, and inserted two fingers into my vagina. He lifted my leg a little, for more access, as he pushed his fingers further inside me from behind. His other arm was under me, and still wrapped tightly around my torso, as he kissed my neck from behind. He switched back and forth between rubbing my clit, and plunging his fingers back inside me. I threw my head back, and he kissed my lips.

"This pussy is tight. You promise you never gave my shit away?" he asked in a low tone.

"I promise," I moaned. "Fuck, Julius," I bit my lip, as he sped up his finger thrusts.

"Tell me you love me," he said.

"I love you so much Ju," I whimpered.

"You about to cum, look at me," he said, knowing my body better than me. He loved to see my face when I was cumming. I did as he asked, and turned to look at him.

"Are you coming back home?" I moaned as I felt myself about to explode.

"Yeah, as soon as you cum for me," he replied and bit my ear.

As soon as he did that, I released onto his fingers. He slid them out slowly, and then licked his them. He slowly inserted his dick, inch by inch, and gripped my torso tight so I couldn't move. He pumped slowly, until he could fit all the way in. He gripped my body tighter, and sucked on my shoulder.

"Aahhh. Mmmmm Julius," I purred, as he plunged his long, thick pole into me.

He gripped my jaw with his hand and leaned my head back for a kiss. He took his other hand and reached in front of me to play with my clit. He had my body locked against his, using one arm, as he feverishly played with my clit using the other. He sped up his pelvic thrusts, beating my shit to a pulp, as he bit my shoulder.

"Ah, fuck Nat!" he damn near yelled into my mouth as he began to suck my lips.

He lifted my leg a little more, using his knee, and sped up some more. We both exploded, and our bodies jerked together as we yelled out. He played with my nipples, as we panted trying to catch our breath.

"Fuck, you got some good shit babe," he grunted as his hands roamed the front of my naked shivering body.

I saw Paula had called me, but I was too spent to call her back.

Later that night, Julius decided to take Jackson and I to this really nice restaurant named Charleston Grill. It was starting to become his routine. Whenever he messed up, he wanted to take me out and buy me things. None of that stuff mattered to me unless he was actually going to be different. At least him agreeing to come home was a start.

I decided to go with a simple red Roberto Cavalli dress. It reminded me of a kimono, but just really short. I let my hair hang down, because I had to spend extra time covering the slight bruising and swelling around my eye. I didn't usually wear makeup, but I had to tonight. Julius was looking fine as usual, in Roberto Cavalli jeans and a grey Cavalli crew neck. I wished they made stuff for babies, but since they didn't, we dressed Jackson in some dark jeans, and a grey crew neck like his daddy.

"You ready baby?" Julius asked with Jackson on his hip. I nodded and got up to walk out the bedroom. Julius rushed after me, and grabbed my waist from behind. He craned his neck around and kissed my lips softly, making me smile.

Charleston Grill was really beautiful, and made me feel like I was dining in a rich uncle's house. It had a homey feeling, with all the wooden walls. The chairs and tables were all white, giving it an expensive feel as well. We didn't wait long to be seated, and once we were, we ordered drinks so I could have something in my stomach.

"I'm sorry for hitting you again baby girl," Julius broke the silence, and adjusted Jackson in his lap.

"I know," I said, not bothering to look up from the menu.

"You still upset?" he asked calmly.

"Yeah," I said, finally looking up.

"What you want me to do? I brought you roses and stuff," he replied with a concerned expression.

"That's nice Julius, but it doesn't matter if you're gonna do the same things."

"You right," he said, and then looked out the window of the restaurant.

We talked for a little bit more over dinner, and the food was as good as I expected. I couldn't wait to get home and get my feet rubbed. I hadn't been pregnant long, but my feet were hurting so bad already.

"Jackson is knocked out," Julius said as he walked into the bedroom.

He walked over and sat next to me on the bed, then exhaled heavily. He pulled me into his lap, and pushed my hair behind my ears. He went into his jacket pocket and pulled out a velvet box. When he opened it, it contained a gold chain, with a gold ring hanging from it.

"Julius, I"

"Just hear me out real quick ma," he exhaled. "I don't know why you love me, but I'm glad that you do. You deserve better than me, but instead of just saying that and letting you go, I'm gonna be the man you've deserved this whole time," he started, and tears were running down my face. I wiped them, and sniffled so I could pay attention. "I want you to wear this, as a symbol of a promise I'm gonna make to you," he smiled and wiped my tears, 'cause I couldn't stop them. He kissed my lips, and then cleared his throat as he tightened his grip around my waist. "I promise you that as long as there is air in my lungs, I will never hit you again. I will never hurt you again, or let anyone else hurt you. I promise that as long as you and I are in a relationship, I will be faithful to you. I want this Natalia, us. I want us and our kids, babe. Yes, the one in your stomach, because I know it's mine. I need you to wear this, so that no matter what's going on, or how you're feeling in a particular moment, you will remember my promise to you. I won't ever break this promise to you. Aight?" he finally smiled.

I couldn't do anything but nod, as he kissed my lips repeatedly. He fastened the necklace around my neck, and then kissed me again. I hugged him tight and melted in his strong embrace.

"No more Bianca?" I smiled.

"What? Woman, hell nah!" he shook his head in disgust, and I chuckled.

"I love you Julius Tate," I said holding his face and looking into his eyes. He kissed me as I sniffled a bit.

"I love you, so, so, so much more Natalia Tate," he replied biting his lip.

I looked at my wedding band and engagement ring, and then chuckled because I was so happy.

Afterwards, my husband gave me a full body massage, with oils included. Once he was done, we indulged in our favorite past time, a bubble bath and my favorite pink champagne, the non-alcoholic version however. Once we were done, we looked through our wedding and honeymoon pictures for the rest of the night.

LUCY

Natalia didn't talk to me for four weeks, but at least she had still been paying my rent. She'd been ignoring my texts and calls constantly, up until about three days ago. At first I couldn't blame her, but then it started to just piss me off. To top it off, Menzo seemed to be ignoring me as well. I bet they were somewhere together, fucking each other. I knew she was alive and well during that four week stint, because she posted a couple pictures of she and Julius at the park with their son. Then she went to dinner with Paula and their kids. I was still furious with Natalia, but I had something for her shady ass now that we were somewhat cool again.

Natalia Bff: *We are here.*

Tonight we were flying to Las Vegas, because we had tickets to see Michael Jackson and the Beatles' Cirque du Soleil show. Natalia's ass knew better than to not invite me this time. Paula was bringing her daughter Gabby, and Natalia was bringing Jackson, so I was bringing Lumar. I really didn't want to take my son, but since Winnie was coming, I decided to. No need for me to pay for my own nanny, when Natalia had one.

"Hey," I said dryly, as I got into the stretch limo. It was a couple other niggas, including Julius' brother Rashad, his friends Tim, Dash, and Leese, and then their females, so I was the only solo one. I was wondering why Menzo wasn't there. "We're driving to Vegas?" I frowned.

"No, flying," Rashad replied.

I nodded and stared out the window, as we drove to the private airport. Once we boarded Julius' private jet, I handed my son, Lumar to Winnie, so she could hold him; I needed my rest. Everyone kind of looked at me, but I didn't give a fuck.

I rolled my eyes when I heard kissing, 'cause I knew it was Julius and Natalia. Originally, I encouraged Natalia's relationship with Julius, because he was just some street hustler. He was sexy as fuck, but there were niggas with way fatter pockets than him. Had I'd known he had plans to shoot to the top and become rich as fuck, I would've went for him myself.

You see, back in Indianapolis, he and Menzo were at the same level, so it didn't matter to me. Julius was better looking, but I had already pushed up on Menzo, and then next thing I knew, Natalia and Julius had a thing. Yeah Menzo made more money with this move to Charleston, but not as much as Julius. Plus, Julius was a boss, and that shit made my panties wet. He was only 21, and had his shit to-fuckin-gether man. And something about him being married now, made me want him even more.

We were staying at the Venetian for four days, and that shit was off the damn chain. What was even better, was the fact that I didn't have to pay a dime. All the guys paid for their Penthouse suites, and Julius paid for mine. Look at him already paying my way, with his sexy ass. I had a suite all to myself, and hopefully I would be sharing it with a certain someone fairly soon.

KNOCK!

KNOCK!

KNOCK!

"You wanna go to the fashion mall with me and Paula?" Natalia asked when I opened the door.

"You bringing him?" I frowned pointing to Jackson on her hip, playing with a gold chain she was wearing.

"Yeah, he's my baby. I like having him with me," she replied sarcastically, and I rolled my eyes.

"Is Lumar with Winnie?" I asked and she nodded.

Paula had her daughter too, but I didn't want to bring my son. I loved him, but I was just going through something right now.

"Well, I don't feel like carrying Lumar," I shook my head and grabbed my purse.

"I have my double stroller," Natalia offered.

"Why do you have a double?" I asked.

"I'm pregnant again, remember?" she smiled.

"Nah, he's good with Winnie," I replied and we headed to the mall.

LATER THAT NIGHT

After the crew got home from a movie and dinner, I relaxed in my room for a bit. I wanted to go check on Julius, so I got dressed again and headed down the hall. I stole their spare key, when I was chilling with Natalia after the mall.

I quietly used the card to enter their room, and closed the door gently. I saw Winnie knocked out in the living room area, and Jackson sleeping on his little pallet-like bed. I heard loud moans in the distance, and a smile crept across my face. I twisted the doorknob to the bedroom slowly, and pushed it open just a little.

Natalia was lying horizontally across the bed with her legs open, and Julius was on the floor with his head between them. She had a baby bump that was very small. All I could see were Julius' sexy shoulders, and it was enough to turn me on.

"Mmmm, Juuuu," she moaned as she slowly wound her hips against his mouth. "Ah! Lucy!" she yelped, snapping me back to life.

I was so into watching them, that I didn't realize Natalia saw me. She covered her small body with a sheet, and Julius started laughing loud as hell.

"You need something Lucy?" Julius frowned and wiped his mouth.

"Uhh, um, no," I stuttered and closed their door. I heard one of them lock it right after.

"She was watching us Julius!" I heard Natalia say in a loud whisper.

"Relaaaax baby girl," he chuckled. "Come here, I wasn't done with you yet," he added.

I heard her moaning a couple seconds later, so I retreated back to my room.

Natalia and Paula went to go walk the strip, but I declined to go this time. I had better things to do this evening. I put on my new lingerie set, and a silk robe. My freshly pressed bob was hanging loosely and looking perfect. I put some bronzer on, and rubbed some Amber Blush lotion all over my smooth vanilla complexion. I was really light, but I was still really sexy. My mother was white and my daddy was black, so I guess that's why I was so fair. I put on some red lipstick and headed down to Natalia and Julius' room.

"Who is it?" Winnie yelled out, after I knocked on the suite door. *Fuck! Think Lucy!*

"Uh, Lucy," I finally replied.

"Oh, Ms. Lucy, you look- you look very"

"Yes, I have a guest down in my suite, but I just need to ask Julius something," I said walking in the room past her.

I smiled when I realized Natalia had taken Jackson with her. I kissed Lumar on his cute little cheek, and then switched my ass to Julius' room. I walked in, and heard him talking on the phone in the bathroom, within the room.

"Nah," he chuckled. "I'll talk to you about it when I get back," he said.

I stayed hidden around the corner so I could listen. I bet that was some hoe he was entertaining, he better get ready to entertain another one though.

"Yeah, I'm in Vegas with my wife. She wanted to see that MJ show, so yeah. Exactly. Hahaha. Aight, peace."

As soon as he said peace, I hit the corner and dropped my robe. "What's up Ju?" I raised a brow, as his eyes roamed my body.

"What's up? What you doing?" he frowned.

"I think you know what I'm doing Julius. The question is what are you gonna do about it?" I smirked as I walked closer to him.

He was fresh out the shower, and his sexy abs, arms, and chest glistened. His honey complexion was perfect, just like his chiseled features, and full lips.

"Oh my gosh," he said throwing his head back, and running a hand over his face. "You wild," he chuckled nervously.

"You right," I chuckled as I ran a finger down his abs.

"Natalia wait ba" he tried to say.

I looked over my shoulder, and Natalia had sprinted out. Julius held onto his towel, and chased after her. I walked out the bathroom slowly, and saw him trying to keep her from leaving the suite.

"Get off me! And take your fucking necklace!" she yelled as she tried to fight him off.

"Winnie, please bring me a pair of boxer shorts!" he yelled out as he tried to restrain Natalia, and keep his towel up at the same time.

I had never seen her this mad, and I was scared to come out. I felt so bad because she was crying her eyes out. Winnie ran into the living room, with some boxers and basketball shorts, and Julius snatched them.

"Thank you," he said as he quickly slipped them on. He had a nice big dick. I smiled for a second at the thought.

As he put on his clothing, Natalia tried to dart past him, but he caught her in time. He rushed her into the wall, and towered over her. She punched him in the nuts, and he collapsed to the floor. He still got up and chased her, then pinned her onto the couch. Jackson was oblivious, making baby noises and playing with his toys in his playpen.

"Calm your ass down Natalia! She pushed up on me! I didn't do shit!" he yelled. She just stared at him, out of breath and sniffling. He kissed her softly, and then sucked her lips. "Baby, please believe me. I just made you a promise. I wouldn't do this shit. Don't stress the baby out," he said in a low tone, as Winnie and I watched, wondering what was to come.

He finally let her wrists go, and she cupped his face to return the kiss. Winnie and I let out a sigh of relief, and I finally felt bold enough to come from behind the bedroom door.

"I love you Nat. Aight?" he said in between kisses.

What the fuck was I doing? Natalia was my best friend. She was like my sister, and this is what I do to her?

She nodded and got up from the couch, then walked up to me. She cocked her fist back, and punched me hard as hell. I flew back into the bedroom, and hit my lower back on the dresser. My nose was gushing blood at an alarming rate, but I wasn't even gonna hit her back 'cause I deserved that.

"I deserved that. I'm sorry you guys," I said before grabbing Lumar, and rushing back to my room.

I needed to get it together.

My operation was moving weight quicker than I'd expected. We were literally running through product on a consistent basis. I had to triple my shipment from Bart, which he said was no problem. However, one of his men got caught flying in part of the shipment, and all of it was confiscated. I had never been more upset in my life. To make matters worse, I had a schedule that I gave to Bart, to let him know what day and time his mule should fly the product in. He was late getting the additional product I needed, so he tried to rush the mule out and when he did, the nigga got caught with my shit.

Bart had been good to me and had never fucked up in the past, but this was some straight bullshit. I wasn't gonna end my relationship over this one incident, although I really wanted to. I just told him to drop my shipment amount back to the original quantity. Why did I do that? 'Cause I got an extra connect.

Antonio Rojas was gonna get me pure cocaine from Columbia, but by submarine. He was closer to South Carolina, and the route was safer. This way, I would have as much cocaine as I needed, without stressing my connects. Antonio claimed he could fulfill my whole order, but I didn't trust him, and I didn't want to kick Bart to the curb because he was like a father to me.

"So does Bart know about Antonio?" my brother Rashad asked, as we watched TV in my den.

"Yeah, I told him. I only said something because he's cool. Otherwise I wouldn't have said shit," I frowned.

"I'm glad you figured some shit out, because that was a lot of fucking weight that was confiscated 'cause of him," Tim scoffed and took a pull on his blunt.

"Nigga, who you telling? I wanted to murk that nigga," I frowned shaking my head. Bart was lucky, 'cause if any other connect had have done that shit, I would've lit they ass up with my AK.

"This submarine shit is genius though bro," Rashad smiled.

"I know right, safe as hell. But y'all know y'all gone have to work separately now, because the shipments are coming on separate days," I informed them. "Y'all each gone have someone with y'all, but you guys are veterans which is why I need y'all separate. Tim, you gone have Luke with you, and Rashad, you gone have Jabari," I added.

Luke and Jabari had proven themselves over the last couple of months, so when I found new positions open, I quickly promoted them. I was happy to see them being able to live better, plus they deserved it. I filled their trap positions with these other cats named Henry and Miles, after their little hood background check cleared. I think I was the only kingpin that did background checks, but it needed to be done. I kept my team small, only putting on as little as possible, because I needed to know every single muthafucka that was pushing my product. Niggas knew I didn't fucking play, so they never even tried me; well the smart ones didn't. I had a sprinkle of niggas try to run game, and they are no longer with us, thanks to Dash and Leese.

Another tactic I had, was building a great relationship with my connects. A good friendship, plus the ability to push weight at a fast pace, always brought positive results. After working with me for a while, I was able to convince them not to supply anybody in South Carolina. I was fucking balling, and it made me smile when I thought about it.

"I made cupcakes for you guys," Natalia appeared with a beautiful smile on her face.

She was holding a tray of her bomb ass blueberry cheesecake cupcakes. Every Saturday night, she made them for me and today was no exception.

"Thanks ma, but you could've had Winnie bring them in" I said as she sat them down on the coffee table in front of Rashad, Tim, and I.

"I'm pregnant, not handicapped Ju," she chuckled and so did we.

"Come here," I said tugging her into my lap. Everyone else kept their eyes glued to the game on the big screen, and stuffed their face with cupcakes.

Natalia had on a simple tan tube dress, and her favorite fuzzy slippers. Her belly was starting to poke out more, but could be passed off as a food baby, and her brown curly hair was hanging down. Her golden complexion reminded me of butter, due to its glowing smooth, look and feel. She smelled like some sweet sugar, and it made me lick my lips. I rubbed her stomach, and she temporarily glanced down to watch me. She played with the gold promise chain and ring I had given her, as she looked at the TV.

"Give me a kiss," I said in a low tone. She turned to me, and pecked me a couple times. She dipped her tongue in my mouth, and I squeezed her butt. "You know I wanna taste that later," I said as we kissed.

"Come on man! We can barely pay attention, with y'all damn near fucking over there!" Rashad turned his lip up.

Natalia chuckled and stood up to leave. I smacked her little fat ass, and bit my lip. I couldn't wait to watch her ride my dick tonight.

"Aye," Rashad started, but made sure Natalia was long gone before he continued. "Bianca out here saying she's pregnant by you dawg." he finished.

"Nigga what!" I frowned and sat up straight.

"Yeah, she told somebody and you know how word gets around. I just wanted you to know before someone tells or mentions it to Natalia," Rashad replied.

"Wait, ain't no way she pregnant by me. I always used a condom.

And I haven't fucked since that time Natalia and I broke up 'cause Menzo lied on her," I said shaking my head in confusion.

"Maybe the condom broke," Tim chuckled and bit another brownie.

"Have you forgotten that I fucked Bianca for two years straight, and she didn't get pregnant before? So how all of a sudden now we're breaking condoms? That bitch better go on somewhere with that," I said shaking my head.

I wasn't worried about that baby being mine; I was worried that my wife would think it was. Natalia knew I was fucking Bianca during that little hiatus we had, and she would believe that rumor in a second. I knew I wouldn't be worth shit if Natalia left me, so I needed to prevent that. I needed to holla at Bianca and see what the fuck she was out here talking about.

Tonight was Paula's 22nd birthday, and we were going back to Raye's Lounge. The only difference about tonight was that our men were coming with us, and Lucy wasn't. She tried calling me and texting me, but I wasn't ready to answer yet.

I really wanted to have fun tonight, because all I had been doing was being a wife and mommy. I planned to start school too, but that wasn't gonna be until next year.

I decided to wear a simple red dress that stopped mid-thigh, with thin straps. I wore matching red stilettoes, the kind where basically your whole foot is out. I put my curly brown hair in a messy bun on my head, and then put on some red lipstick.

"Mmm, what perfume is that?" Julius asked as he hugged me from behind.

"Daisy, by Marc Jacobs," I smiled.

"Smells good as hell," he said, sniffing my neck from behind.

"Thank you," I smiled.

Julius was wearing light blue jeans, a red varsity jacket, a white t-shirt, and red tubular Adidas. He wore his usual Dolce and Gabanna cologne, which always made my nipples hard. Anytime I smelled that cologne, I thought of him. When we were broken up, the smell made me sad. When we were good, the smell made me happy.

"What you thinking about?" he asked as he sipped a cup of Jack Daniels.

"Us," I replied putting on my earring.

"What about us?" he asked sitting on the bed.

"Just that, I hope it stays how it is now," I replied turning away from the mirror to him.

He grabbed my hand and pulled me over to him. I was standing between his legs, as he held onto my waist.

"I was serious when I gave you that thing around your neck babe. We gone be good, don't worry," he smiled and kissed my small baby bump. "Okay?"

"Okay," I smiled and blushed. I wrapped my arms around his neck, and hugged him tight.

We arrived to Raye's Lounge around 10pm, and it was live as hell. I wasn't sure why they called it a lounge, when after 9:30 it was a full on club. "Again" by Young Thug was playing, and people were dancing hard as hell. Julius was like my bodyguard, and it was so cute. He was scared someone would hit me in the stomach. We finally got to the VIP booth, and I saw Paula dancing on Rashad with a crown on her head. There was glitter all over her pretty brown skin, and she had on a sheer black dress. It was long in the back and short in the front, showing her thick, toned legs.

"Heyyy boo!" Paula screamed, and pushed her long dark hair behind her shoulder before hugging me.

"Happy Birthday!" I said handing her a gift, as Julius dapped up his brother and other homies.

"Thank you beautiful. I like that bracelet!" she said touching my wrists.

"Thank you," I chuckled. "Husband got it for me yesterday," I smiled and touched the iced out bracelet.

"Damn bitch. That along with your wedding ring has that hand rocking at least a couple million," she smirked.

"Million?" I frowned.

"Girl yes!" she bucked her eyes, and laughed as she swayed her body to the music.

I looked over at Julius, 'cause I was surprised he spent that much money on me. I walked over to him as "100" by The Game and Drake played. He was texting on his phone when I got to him, and the screen was lighting up his face in the dark club. I barged my way into his lap, to give him a nice little lap dance.

"You better stop with your little sexy ass," he whispered in my ear.

"Stop? Why?" I chuckled.

"Cause you making me wanna take you back home," he replied, as he wrapped his arm around my waist. I finished my little dance, and I could feel his hard dick on my butt.

The party had been going on for a little while, and I was starting to get hungry as hell. I was gently swaying to the music, while still in Julius' lap. He was texting still, and lightly rubbing my small stomach. I looked over to my left, and spotted Marlon and one of his homies walking into the VIP area. *God please no*, I thought as I tried to keep looking without being seen. Unfortunately, Marlon spotted me and stared in disappointment for a bit, when he saw me sitting in Julius' lap. He was wearing a silk shirt, with skinny jeans, and Nikes. I didn't like his outfit at all, but hey, he ain't my nigga. I mean, Julius didn't wear super baggy jeans either, but this nigga's jeans were suffocating his balls. He nodded his head to say what's up, and I half smiled.

"I have to go to the bathroom babe, you gone be okay?" Julius asked, as he lightly moved me off his lap.

"Yeah, I will," I replied.

As soon as he left, Marlon made his way over to me.

"Hey beautiful," he smiled.

"Hi Marlon," I replied and half smiled again.

"You ain't been getting my texts or calls, Ms. Natalia?" he asked smiling. He was still cute as fuck.

"Yes, but I'm married now. Didn't I tell you?" I asked and smiled.

"No, but damn," he said immediately directing his attention to my blinding ring finger. "To that guy whose lap you was sitting on?"

"Take a wild guess Marlon," I replied laughing. "The same guy who kicked you out that day." I added.

"You are so beautiful Natalia, damn," he said shaking his head and staring into my eyes.

"Thanks," I responded in a low tone, as I played with the gold ring band on my necklace.

"I would love to still take you out, just once. I feel like you owe me, 'cause I've been asking since before you ran off and got your bad ass married," he smiled.

"No, Marlon I"

"Come on ma," he pleaded leaning his face close to mine, and looking deeply into my eyes.

Suddenly, someone tapped his shoulder, and when he turned around, Julius punched his ass. Everyone started moving out the way, and people outside of VIP ran over to watch as Julius and Marlon fought.

"Julius, stop, you"

"Back up baby girl, you're pregnant," Rashad said standing in front of me.

Marlon had passed out after the rumble, and the police were making their way through. They barged into VIP, and handcuffed Julius, as I screamed, cried, and tried to fight my way past Rashad. Someone stood over Marlon, and started slapping his face until he finally came to.

"Aye Tim, come here," Rashad yelled over the commotion, as the police escorted Julius through the crowd.

Tim walked over, and picked me up bridal style to carry me out, while Rashad escorted Paula. We piled into Rashad's Range Rover, and followed the police car. I was crying my eyes out, as I peered through the front windshield from the backseat. I wanted to make sure Rashad was following the police car close enough.

"Relax ma-ma," Paula said rubbing my stomach.

My bump wasn't even that big, but people were acting like I was eight months. I was only like four. Nonetheless, I sat back, and took a deep breath. New tears stopped producing from my eyes, as I stared out my own window.

We finally got to where the police was holding Julius, and I rushed inside past everyone. I ran up to the little desk where an officer was sitting, and panted out of breath.

"Can I help you young lady?" he asked.

"Yes, my husband was just brought in here and"

"Go sit down, and relax Natalia. I got it." Rashad came up behind me, and pulled me away by my waist. I paused for a second, and then went to sit down.

Rashad talked to the officer a little bit, as I watched closely. I kept looking at every guy that walked by, making sure it wasn't Julius. Finally, Rashad walked away from the desk and stood in front of Tim, Paula, and I.

"So they verified that Marlon was okay, so they are gonna release Julius right now. We just had to pay $8,000. He should be coming out in a little bit," he exhaled.

We waited about thirty minutes, and finally Julius emerged from the back. He looked untouched, and just as sexy as when we left the house. He walked out the police station, and all of us followed. Rashad walked over and greeted him, as well as Tim and Paula. I walked behind them slowly, 'cause I knew Julius wanted to kill me. I didn't even want to think about the ass whooping he was gonna deliver to me. Everyone piled into the car but Julius, and I slowly walked over to him. He took his hands out his jacket pockets and I lightly flinched.

"Come here girl," he said pulling my arm. He towered over me and cupped my face. He kissed my lips, surprising me, and then stared me in the eyes. "You and my baby okay?" he asked.

"Yeah," I nodded. I was in disbelief that he wasn't beating my ass.

"Good, I'm sorry," he half-smiled and kissed me again. "I should've just told that nigga to get out your face, but when I saw him, I just got angry," he added.

"It's okay," I chuckled nervously.

"Don't be scared of me anymore baby, I'm here to protect you aight?" he raised a brow, and I nodded and smiled. I stood on my tiptoes, and cupped his face for a deep kiss.

He turned around and opened Rashad's back door for me, then climbed in after me. I was still skeptical, thinking he was only being nice 'cause we were outside a police station; however, when we got home, we just made love and went to bed. I guess he really meant it when he said he wasn't gonna hit me anymore, and I was thankful.

JULIUS

I hit up Bianca and told her to meet me at my warehouse. No, I wasn't gone kill her ass, but I didn't need any nosey muthafuckas seeing us out and telling Natalia. For the first time in my life, I had a woman that I was terrified of losing, so I would do what was needed to prevent that.

As I sat inside the warehouse, I heard a car pulling up. I had Dash go stand by the door, so he could give Bianca a good little pat down before coming in to see me. If she was crazy enough to go around pinning a baby on me, she was crazy enough to come in here with guns blazing.

I heard the sound of heels clicking against the floor, and soon enough Bianca appeared. She was wearing jeans and a tight ass t-shirt. She sat down across from me, and put her big ass Gucci purse in her lap.

"Hey Ju," she said licking her full lips.

"Aight, so I'm gone get straight to the point B, why are you out here saying you having my baby?" I frowned.

"Cause that's the truth," she replied. "I'm two months." she added and rubbed her stomach.

"Bianca, it's me, Julius. You know I ain't falling for that shit," I said.

"You ain't got to fall for something that's true."

"Let me ask you this. How is it you never got pregnant during the two years we were together?" I asked.

"I don't know. I ain't no damn doctor!" she spat.

"Lower your voice Bianca," I said sternly, and she hunched her shoulders. "You never got pregnant because we used condoms every single time. We've always used condoms," I frowned.

"Well how the hell did you get Natalia pregnant then?" she raised a brow.

"Because I raw dogged her Bianca! I've never used a condom with Natalia, ever!" I bucked my eyes.

"Are you telling me that you was sticking your dick in her with no protection, and then coming home to me and getting head?" she frowned. She was always tryna make shit be about our old ass relationship.

"Okay, I never came home to you for one. But like I said, the condom drawer wasn't even opened when I fucked Natalia" I said nonchalantly.

"Wow. How many other bitches did you fuck raw while we were together nigga?" she glared at me, as her eyes became watery.

"Only Natalia, but that's not the fucking point. You"

"Not the fucking point? I was so fucking stupid for your ass! All that time I tried to believe you were just smashing that little hoe on the side, when that wasn't even the case! You were out here eating her pussy and fucking her raw, like I wasn't your damn girlfriend! Ahhhh! Doing shit with her, that you wasn't doing with me! Your actual girlfriend nigga!!!" she screamed.

"Calm down Bianca, you bringing up old shit for no reason." I shook my head.

"It's old to you, but not to me because I love you. Did you ever even love me?" she cocked her head to the side.

"Bianca"

"Did you Julius? I just wanna know."

"No, I didn't," I replied.

Before I could finish the sentence, she broke down into tears. I picked my chair up, then went and sat next to her. I hugged her, and rubbed her back as I shook my head. I just needed her to stop spreading lies; I didn't have time for this Jerry Springer show shit.

"Why Julius? What did I do wrong?" she cried.

"Nothing, I guess it just never happened for me," I shrugged.

"Why Natalia?" she asked.

"I don't know Bianca," I replied not trying to hurt her feelings. I couldn't have her spreading these baby lies around the city, so if answering her dumb ass questions or sugar coating shit would get me on her good side, then so be it.

"You know Julius. What made her better?" she sniffled, staring at me.

I exhaled heavily, and looked at my watch. "Natalia is self-sufficient. She doesn't have to use her body to get by. It may not be good what she does in order to make ends meet, but she will make it happen. She's beautiful and sexy as hell, obviously. But most of all, she's genuine. She's a sweet person, and always puts others before herself. She has my back like no one else in this world, and she loves me despite my many demons. Everything is unconditional with her. She is just what every man wants, in a girlfriend, a wife, just everything. I'm really lucky to be her husband," I finally replied nodding my head.

"I see," she scoffed and dropped her head. "My love wasn't unconditional? I stuck by you through all the shit you did!" she picked her head up and glared at me.

"No, you let me disrespect you," I replied.

"So you ain't never cheated on Natalia? Nigga please!"

"You're right, I have, but she wasn't sitting at home knowing I was fucking other bitches. She thought I was being faithful. You knew I wasn't."

"She thinks you're faithful now?" she raised an eyebrow.

"Yeah, and I am," I responded honestly

"Woooow," she threw her head back. "This bitch must have gold in her pussy!"

"She does," I nodded and pursed my lips.

"I see," she said, wiping her tear stained face.

"But look Bianca, you gotta stop going around saying that's my baby."

"Why, so your precious little Natalia won't get upset?" she frowned.

"Well yes, but also because you and I both know it's a damn lie," I said. I was starting to get irritated.

"Or maybe it's not. This is your baby Julius, and you need to figure out a way to tell your little girlfriend!" she said standing up.

"That's my wife," I corrected her. "And Bianca, don't make this hard for yourself. You don't want to be an enemy of mine."

"Got it King Julius," she fake smiled and switched off. "Oh and by the way, I still love you daddy. I won't ever give up on us. You can come home whenever you want," she smiled.

I closed my eyes and let my head fall back. That was the biggest waste of time ever. Why did I think I could have a civil conversation, with a bitch that would lie and say she was having my baby? I should've known she wasn't all there, when she followed me here from Indianapolis.

BIANCA EVANS

Julius was the only nigga I could ever love. I just couldn't allow him to run off into the sunset with Natalia. Was he crazy? We were together for two years, and he threw all that away for a bitch he'd only known a couple months. That was some bullshit. She must've been into some voodoo, because the Julius Christian Tate I knew, would never marry any bitch nor even try to be faithful. I was the only girl who could accept him the way he was and he knew that.

I'm sure you're wondering if I'm actually pregnant by Julius. I'm not pregnant by Julius, or anyone for that matter. There is no baby. Well, there is no baby anymore. You see, Menzo got me pregnant, but I knew I couldn't keep it if I wanted to be with Julius. Julius wouldn't dare accept a baby from another man, especially his homeboy. I only fucked with Menzo because he said he would help me get Julius back. He was in love with Natalia, and he knew if he made Julius think they had something going on, he would leave her. Over time we developed feelings for one another, but not enough for me to keep his baby or the chlamydia he gave me. Nasty muthafucka. I'm glad I didn't fuck with him like that though, because that nigga disappeared on me, just like Daphne.

Speaking of that grimy bitch, I sent her here to Charleston to do a job, and that bitch got ghost. She told me she had done it, but then I never heard from her again. It seemed like anybody I sent to do a damn job, ended up dipping out. Maybe Julius was paying them off.

Hearing Julius tell me he was smashing Natalia raw this whole time, made me sick to my stomach. I don't know if it was because he was sticking that same dick in my mouth, or because he had feelings strong enough for her that he would risk getting her pregnant. This married, faithful, father Julius, was not the man I knew, but he was the man I always wanted him to be. The fact that he changed and matured for his little Natalia, made him more attractive. See, I'm sure she thought him changing was a good thing for her, when in actuality it was about to get worse.

Julius was always *that* nigga, and bitches were always ready to drop their panties for him at any given moment. But now that he's all mature and shit, bitches gone want him even more. It's nothing more attractive than a boss ass nigga, who can be a King at home as well as in the streets. Natalia started off with a piece of gold, but he turned into a fucking diamond. Now that I knew Julius actually could commit, there was no other option in life but he and I being together.

I wasn't pregnant, but I was gonna have a baby somehow, and it was gonna be Julius'. If this didn't run little miss Natalia off, then I would agree to share him, but not having him was not an option. I enjoyed the show *Sister Wives*, and I'm sure I could get used to a situation of the sort. I'd do anything for Julius, anything.

"So all I need from you is sonogram pictures and things like that," I said to this chick named Lizzie.

Lizzie was my homegirl who was three months pregnant, and I was paying her to cover for me with Julius. Anytime he planned to get suspicious of my pregnancy, she was gonna come through. She had already peed in a couple cups for me, in case he demanded I pee on a stick. Whenever she had a doctor's appointment, she was gonna give me a copy of the sonogram picture. I chuckled out loud at my thoughts. This shit was gone be perfect.

"Okay, so this payment schedule, when is that gonna take place?" Lizzie asked.

"We agreed on $2,000, right?" I smiled.

"Yes," she smiled back.

"I will give you $300 a month."

"Three-hundred dollars a month? Bianca, that can take up to 7 months almost!" she frowned.

"Look! I told you my boyfriend is crazy and he needs to know I'm pregnant. If you fuck this up, he will kill you."

"Okay, $300 is fine," she replied.

"I know it is," I said taking a pull on a blunt.

I couldn't wait to see this play out.

2 MONTHS LATER

"Okay Mr. and Mrs. Tate, are we ready to find out what we're having?" my doctor Theresa asked, as she put the cold jelly on my belly.

"Yes, we are," I smiled and looked at Julius, who was holding Jackson.

"Alright, so it looks like this one isss... a girl," she smiled. "Is that what we wanted?" she asked.

"Yeah," Julius and I said in unison.

"I would take another boy though," he added and we laughed.

I wanted a daughter so bad, now that I already had a boy. Julius and I already had a name picked out for her and everything, so this was perfect.

After we left the doctor, we decided to go out to eat to celebrate. I had a taste for Fiery Ron's barbecue again, so we decided to go there. I realized I only ate there when I was pregnant, but they were good regardless.

"Are you excited to have a little girl?" I smiled and sipped my drink.

"I hope she is like her mother, and not these other hoes out here," Julius joked.

"I hope she is better than me," I chuckled.

"Nah, you're perfect baby girl," he smiled and kissed the back of my hand.

"I love you Julius," I smiled. "And you too baby," I said kissing Jackson's cheek. Julius half-smiled at the two of us for a moment, before speaking.

"What do you mean when you say you love me?" he asked.

"What?"

"Like what does it mean to you, to be in love with me?" he questioned, and then the waitress set down our plates.

"Umm, it means that I care about you, I wanna make you happy, I got your back, that I would do anything for you, and that I will stick by your side no matter what," I replied.

"No matter what?" he raised an eyebrow.

"Why, what did you do?" I asked in a low tone.

"Nothing baby, I was just making sure I understood," he nodded.

"Oh, well, yeah no matter what. You can tell that by now, right?" I smiled.

"Right."

"Same question for you," I smiled.

"When I say I love you, that means that I'm here for you, I'm gonna protect you, that I care about your well-being more than my own, I enjoy making you happy and being in your presence. That, I wanna be with you for as long as you will allow me to, and that you're beautiful and sexy as fuck." He chuckled at the last part and so did I.

"And that's no matter what?" I smiled.

"That's no matter what baby," he replied sipping his drink.

"Don't ever leave me ma," Julius said as he lay between my legs, with his dick still inside me.

We'd just finished making love, and the room had no light except for the moon shining through the windows. You couldn't see much, but you could see just enough.

"I won't," I said cupping his face.

"You promise?" he asked sucking my lips, and then kissing my neck.

"I promise. Why Julius?" I asked worried. I could tell something was bothering him, and I needed to know what it was.

"I just need to know…that you gone always stick by me," he half-smiled and rubbed my hair.

"I will" I whispered and he cut me off by tonguing me down.

His dick hardened inside me and he started to stroke me slowly. He wrapped his arms tightly around my torso, making sure to not press against my small belly, and continued to pump into me. I had completely forgotten about our little conversation, as he took my body to new heights.

I was losing my fucking mind. My mind was literally on it's way out the damn door. Bianca was insisting that she was pregnant by me, and would not let up. She was so adamant about it, that I was starting to believe her. I've never known her to sleep around, so when she said she had only been with me, I believed her.

I know I should be thinking about my child on the way, but all I cared about right now was not losing Natalia and my kids. I was feeling like this baby was ruining my life, and I didn't want to feel that way if it *was* mine.

"So what you gone do man?" my brother Rashad asked, as we sat in his living room. The only reason I was here was because Paula was gone. I knew she would eavesdrop and tell Natalia anything she heard if she *was* here.

"Man, I don't know. This can't be happening right now," I replied sipping my beer.

"You believe her? Tell that hoe you need some type of proof," Rashad frowned and shook his head.

"I did, and she said she had some. She asked me to come see her today."

"Damn, so that's why you tripping out all of a sudden?" he asked and I nodded. "I mean, what could she have? Ain't like she got a DNA test already."

"Yeah, but you know Bianca ain't never been no hoe my nigga," I scoffed.

"She was pretty loyal, but bitches change Ju. When a woman is angry, they turn into different people," Rashad said trying to ease my mind.

"Yeah I know. Is it bad that the only thing I care about right now is Natalia and my babies?"

"Hell nah man! Stop beating yourself up my nigga. Until you get some papers saying that baby is yours, you ain't got nothing to worry about. You rich, and got a beautiful wife and son with a daughter on the way. Bianca ain't no fucking factor right now. Enjoy your life until you get to that bridge."

"I hear you," I nodded, and my phone buzzed.

Bianca: *I'm home babe.*

Me: *Aight.*

I wished she would stop with the terms of endearment.

"Aight bro, I'm about to go see what Bianca talking about. Please don't forget to *not* mention this shit around Paula," I said while dapping him up.

"Nigga, get yo' ass outta here," he said looking at me like I was crazy, and I laughed.

"Hey Ju," Bianca smiled as she stood behind her door. She had a small round stomach, and it made me sick to even look at it.

"Sup," I said walking into her little apartment.

It was nice and clean, which wasn't a surprise. Bianca was always a damn neat freak. That shit came in handy when she would clean up my crib back in Indianapolis.

"So what you got to show me?" I asked as I sat down on the couch.

"You look nice. You smell good," she smiled and sat next to me.

"Bianca."

"Okay, damn," she said and then dug into her purse. "You said you needed proof, so here you go." She handed me a black and white picture, while rubbing her stomach.

I grabbed the picture, and saw it was one of those ultrasound things. I only knew what it was, because Natalia always kept them and showed them to me. As much as I wanted to believe that Bianca's baby wasn't mine, I knew it was. Bianca didn't fuck around, and I was the only one hitting when she came here to Charleston. Unless she was mother Mary, that was my kid. The days of me denying babies was long gone.

I handed Bianca back the picture and dropped my hand into my hands. I exhaled heavily, as I silently prayed for this to be a nightmare I could wake up from. I'd been telling myself she was faking it, but now I had proof right in front of me.

"What's wrong babe?" Bianca asked as she rubbed my back.

I sat up, and looked over at her. She was still pretty, with her bright red hair, light vanilla skin, and thick ass body.

"Stop calling me babe Bianca," I replied nonchalantly.

"So, now that we have a baby on the way, what are your plans?" she asked caressing her stomach. I hated to see her do that.

"We not doing anything until the baby gets here," I said remembering what Rashad told me.

"So when do you plan to tell Natalia?" she cocked her head to the side.

"Not until I get the DNA results back."

"Wow, so in the meantime when I need something from you, I can't call?" she asked as if she was offended.

"No, I mean… I don't fucking know Bianca, damn!" I frowned.

"You acting like you don't want this baby!" she yelled.

"I don't! I don't want to be tied to you B! When I left you in Indianapolis, I wanted that to be the end!" I yelled back. I was overwhelmed and frustrated as fuck.

"A baby is a blessing Julius! Don't do this!" she shouted and her voice was shaking.

"Bianca, I am married ma! Married! The only time it's a blessing is when it's with my wife."

"Julius, baby relax. We can do this," she said rubbing my fade.

"Bianca, have you not been able to understand that I'm married? Like not a joke marriage but on some real shit. Natalia is my wife ma. Not my girlfriend, not some freak of the week, but my wife. Do you get that?" I squinted my eyes as I looked into hers.

She stared into my eyes, and I could tell she was letting my words sink in. This was the first time she was realizing that what Natalia and I had, was real and forever.

"No, no. I get it," she finally said in a somber tone.

"Good. I'll check up on you here and there, and then once the baby gets here, we will test it. Then I will talk to Natalia if need be," I said standing up, and walking to the door.

"Sounds like a plan," she nodded while wiping a single tear.

Tonight was Rashad's 24th birthday, and it was gonna be a big shindig. Everyone was invited damn near, except me. But, I was able to be someone's plus one, so I was gonna be there anyway. I had a surprise for a couple of the guests that would make tonight one to remember. I always liked Rashad, so I hated to do this at his birthday party, but it was the only time it could happen.

I stood in front of my full-length mirror, and strapped my prosthetic baby bump around my torso. I paid almost $300 for this, because it was silicone. That way, if anybody hugged me or rubbed it, it would feel real. I pulled my turtleneck sweater over it and smiled. I stared at it for a bit, wishing I really were pregnant by Julius. My ringing phone snapped me back to reality, so I answered it right away.

"I'm outside," this girl named Dawn said into the phone.

"K. Coming," I replied before disconnecting.

Dawn thought I was actually pregnant. Only person that knew I wasn't pregnant, was Lizzie, and of course myself. I didn't need word getting back to Julius, so I put up a front for everyone I came in contact with. Plus, being able to park in the pregnancy parking spots when I went out, was always a positive.

"Hey girl. You're getting big," Dawn commented as I got into the car.

"Yeah, I know," I replied dryly.

She didn't even know me like that. I'd just met her like a week ago. Only reason she let me be her plus one, was because I said I could hook her up with Julius' boy, Leese.

We got to this big ass venue, and you could hear "0-100" by Drake, all the way outside. The security guard checked us off on the list, and then let us in. There were two bars on each sides of the room, and then a huge table of cupcakes. I walked over to the cupcake table, because it had "Natalia's Cupcakes" above it. So this bitch can bake? Hilarious. I picked up the one that was beer-maple-brown sugar flavor, and bit into it. Unfortunately, it was probably one of the best cupcakes I'd ever had.

"This shit is bomb! Isn't Natalia Julius' wife?" Dawn asked biting into her cupcake.

"Not really. She trapped him with a baby, so he feels like he needs to be with her," I replied swaying to "Twist My Fingaz" by YG.

"Damn, for real? Grimy ass bitch," she replied, shaking her head and stuffing her face.

"Right?" I said cracking up at my lies.

I scanned the room looking for Natalia and Julius, since I had yet to see them. I grabbed another cupcake that was watermelon lemonade flavor, and it was too damn good; more reasons for me to hate this little bitch. As "Planes" by Jeremih and J.Cole came on, I finally spotted Natalia, standing in front of Julius and lightly dancing on him. She wore a black tube dress that hugged her small body. She was small but always had a nice little shape. Julius had on a black shirt and snapback, with light blue jeans, and black retro Jordan 7s. He had his hands wrapped around her, rubbing her belly. I turned my lip up, when I saw people coming up to her about them good ass cupcakes.

After about twenty minutes of me hiding out, Natalia finally walked away towards what looked like the bathroom. I rushed through the crowd of people to catch up to her. As hard as I was bumping into people, if I actually was pregnant, this baby would be beat the fuck up. I finally caught up to her, but slowed down so she could go into the bathroom first. After she went inside, I counted to twenty, and then followed her in. I listened to her pee, as I found stuff to do in the mirror. I heard the bathroom stall door being unlocked, and took a deep breath. Showtime Bianca.

"Natalia," I smiled as she walked up to the sink.

"Oh, h-hi Bianca," she stammered.

I had to give it to hershe was beautiful as hell. Her golden honey complexion and full lips were to die for. I always tried to tan in order to accomplish that complexion, but it never worked. I looked at her wedding ring and band, and it caused a lump to form in my throat.

"Hey, so, I was wondering if you could send Julius a message for me," I said.

"What kind of message?" she asked as she dried her hands.

"Well as you can see, I'm pregnant like you. Julius is the father, and he's been ignoring me. I don't deserve to be alone, especially when we made this baby together," I said looking as sad as I could. Julius is going to murder me. I thought to myself.

"Your baby is with Julius?" she asked with a concerned expression.

"Yes, how many months are you?" I quizzed her while smiling.

"Seven months," she replied. I was slightly stunned, because she was so little.

"Oh, I'm eight months," I said to ruffle her feathers. "Looks like I was pregnant first. But deliver that message for me okay?" I smiled and left the bathroom.

I waited on the sidelines, and she came storming out. I followed her as close as I could, without her noticing, all the way back to Julius. I stood near, where I could hear and see them perfectly, but not vice versa. She walked over and sat between Julius and Rashad's new bitch, Paula. Julius leaned over to kiss her neck, and she moved out the way. I chuckled to myself, knowing my plan worked perfectly.

"Whats wrong baby girl?" Julius frowned. Tonight was Rashad's birthday, and we were out celebrating.

"You tell me, you liar," I replied.

He turned me to face to him, and I snatched away.

"Natalia? What the fuck is wrong with you?" he asked.

"Bianca is having your baby?" I raised a brow. He paused for a couple seconds, confirming what she had told me. "Wow Julius," I said shaking my head. I was ready to go at this point.

"How did you find out?" he finally asked.

"Doesn't matter," I said standing up. "Can you take me home?"

"Nah, we not going home right now," he replied and bobbed his head to the music.

"Fine, I will find a ride," I said walking off. He grabbed my arm and lightly tugged me back.

"We're not leaving right now," he said.

I snatched my arm from him and stormed off. I didn't know why I acted like I had a ride, when I knew I didn't. Paula rode with Rashad, and I knew he wouldn't take me home. I looked over to my right, and spotted Lucy. She was standing by the wall, swaying to the music with a drink in her hand. She looked so pretty, and I realized I missed her.

She wore a bustier top, skinny jeans, a long sheer cardigan covered in flowers, and black pumps. Her black bob was freshly done, and one side was swooped across like Aaliyah, but pushed behind her ear. Her fair complexion was blemish free as usual. She saw me looking and waved me over.

"What?" I asked when I got close.

"I miss you Nat. I need you to forgive me," she said with pleading eyes.

"I don't know," I said folding my arms. I looked over my shoulder, and saw Julius charging towards me. "Can you give me a ride home Lucy?" I asked as if I was in a rush.

"Sure Nat. Come on," she replied smiling.

We walked out the party hand in hand, and it reminded me of the old days. Once we got outside, the cool air felt good against my skin. The party was hot, so outside was like a heaven right now.

"Natalia!" Julius called out, as he jogged towards us.

I tried to keep walking, but he grabbed my arm. Lucy let my hand go and paused. She looked at Julius and me, and then started to walk off.

"I will be in the car Nat," she smiled and then walked off.

"What Julius? I have to go!" I yelled.

"Watch your fucking mouth Natalia," he said in a low tone as he neared me. I just looked away and folded my arms. "I don't even know if that baby is mine," he added.

"You never think anyone's baby is yours Julius," I replied frowning.

"Baby, that was different. With you, I was in denial. With her, I just don't think it can be possible."

"Did you fuck her?"

"Yeah I did but"

"Okay, so how isn't it possible? Then you got her pregnant right before you married me!" I started to cry.

"What? No I did not ma. We was married already when I- okay wait, it was when"

"Just stop Julius," I said putting my hand up. I started to walk away, but he hugged me from behind.

"Don't do this Natalia. Remember, no matter what? You said no matter what," he whispered in my ear, as he rubbed my belly. "You my wife, the one I love. I only want you baby," he continued.

Tears slid down my cheeks, as I placed my hands on top of his. He kissed my neck, then turned me around to face him. He grabbed my face and started to kiss me passionately. My tears hit my lips, but he didn't care, as he continued to suck them and dip his tongue in my mouth.

"No, stop," I said lightly pushing him away. "I will move to the condo tomorrow," I said looking down.

"Nat"

"No Julius, I need a break right now. This is too much. It's always something with you. You can never just be what I need you to be," I replied with tears racing down my cheeks.

"Natalia, come on ma. I'm changing. This is old baby. I'm trying," he pleaded.

"I just need some time, that's all."

"Time for what baby girl?" he frowned his sexy face up.

"To think... to process this."

"Then you will come back to me?" he asked in a hopeful tone.

"Yeah," I lied. I didn't know what I planned to do just yet. But if telling him I would come back was gonna allow me to be alone for a bit, then I would say it.

"Aight, but nah, I will go to the condo, and you stay at the house. You shouldn't have to move around," he said.

I nodded and walked to Lucy's car. She tried talking to me on the way to my home, but I wasn't in the mood. I could still see her in that lingerie, trying to fuck my husband. Once I saw her pulling up our long driveway, I let out a sigh of relief. I couldn't wait to get away from her and my thoughts. I was gonna take a hot bath, and go to sleep.

"Oh, Natalia, I was thinking we could maybe go to lunch sometime," Lucy smiled.

"I will think about it," I replied and closed her car door before she could say anything else.

Once I was in my pajamas, I picked up my phone to text Julius. *No Natalia.* I told myself. Why couldn't he just be everything he said he would be? How could he go out and get another girl pregnant, and then ask me to marry him? I put my phone down and decided against calling him. I rubbed my belly, and smiled at the fact that I was having a daughter, when my phone rang. I rolled my eyes when I saw it was Julius.

"Hello?" I answered.

"I just wanted to say goodnight," he replied. I smiled and sunk down under the covers, after cutting off my lamp.

"You could've text that."

"I know but I wanted to hear your voice."

"Did you think about hearing my voice when you got Bianca pregnant?" I asked.

"Natalia, I didn't plan this shit. I'm just as shocked as you are."

"But you've known long before tonight I'm sure," I frowned.

"I have, but I wanted to get a DNA test before saying anything."

"Well goodnight Ju," I exhaled.

"Goodnight baby girl. I love you, and let me know if you guys need anything, aight?"

"K," I replied and hung up.

A part of me believed that Julius was telling the truth and that Bianca was up to something. Then again, maybe I was only feeling that way because I wanted to. I had been so stupid for Julius in the past, and my pride wouldn't let me be blind this time.

JULIUS

Bianca had pissed me off by running her fucking mouth to Natalia. I was no longer gonna be nice to her ass. She caused the very thing that I didn't want to happen, to actually happen. I called her phone, and she said she was home already. She sounded like she was happy as hell, and that only made me more upset.

I parked across the street from her apartment complex, and text her to come down. I was not in the mood to be in her place. I wanted this conversation to be quick, and to the fucking point.

"Hey," she said getting in my car. She looked as if she was trying to hold in a laugh, as she stared straight ahead.

"So, what the fuck was the point in running your mouth to Natalia? I told yo' hard headed ass that we were gonna wait until I got a DNA test!" I yelled.

"Because I was tired of being your secret! It's not fair Ju, I loved you for two years!" she yelled back.

"So what! So fucking what Bianca! What we have is over! I've been with Natalia for two years now, as well! We hit two years a month ago!" I yelled and was surprised that I actually remembered the day Nat and I got together.

"You're going through a phase right now, Julius. I mean, who is this girl? You run into her at CVS, and then all of sudden, you push me to the side? This is crazy Julius! Don't you see that! We were in love and"

"Bianca stop it. You and I were never in love. We were nothing more than two people fucking. To be honest, we were just fuck buddies who somehow became boyfriend and girlfriend. If anything, what we had was crazy," I replied shaking my head.

"Julius, stop talking like that! I'm"

"No, you stop acting like you and I are gonna be together. Whether that baby is mine or not Biancano look at me," I stopped and turned her to face me. "Whether that baby is mine or not, you and I will never be together again. If Natalia and I break up for good, I will shed blood, sweat, and tears trying to get her back. And if I can't, I will move on to someone else, not you. I will never be with you again. There is nothing you can say, and there are no amount of babies you can have, that will make you and I, an us," I said as I looked deeply into her eyes.

A million tears seemed to be running down her cheeks, as she started to breathe heavily. She dropped her head in her hands, to get it all out. I exhaled and looked out my window, 'cause I couldn't keep doing this shit with her. I was trying my hardest not to put her 6ft under, but she was making it hard.

"I just don't understand where I went wrong Ju"

"Bianca, stop. I'm tired of this shit. I'm bored with this shit. I'm tired of seeing your name flash across my phone. I'm tired of hearing your voice and seeing your face; I'm just tired. I don't want anything to do with you. I don't believe that is my child, and once we prove that, I want you to act like you don't know me." I finally said what I'd wanted to say to her. I was tired of walking on eggshells and trying not to hurt her damn feelings. I possibly lost my family at this point, so fuck her.

She stared at me and then tugged on the handle of my car to get out. She stood in the doorway of my passenger side, and paused for a couple seconds.

"I will give you some time to come around," she finally said before slamming my door.

As she walked away, I immediately blocked her number in my phone. Just when I did, a text from Franceska came through.

Franceska: *I miss you.*

I shook my head and cranked up my car to head to the condo. When they say your past catches up with you, boy were they telling the truth.

NATALIA

2 WEEKS LATER

"Okay baby," I said out of breath, as I lifted Jackson from the bath.

He was getting heavier, and heavier, and I felt like and my stomach was getting bigger and bigger. I was so used to Julius always picking him up for me, but I refused to call him for help. I made sure to bring his damn stroller everywhere, because carrying him around the grocery store and other places was a no go without Julius.

I dressed my baby, and then put him in his playpen in his room. I turned up his baby monitor, even though I knew Winnie was watching him. I took the other one with me to my daughter's nursery, so I could get back to working on her crib.

I pulled out the manual and started to look over how to build it, when my phone rang.

"Hello?"

"Good afternoon sexy," Marlon spoke into the phone.

"Hi Marlon," I replied dryly.

Somehow, he'd found out that Julius and I split, and he was calling and texting me non-stop. I was always giving him dry responses, or barely texting back, so I wasn't sure why he was continuing to pursue me. He wasn't an ugly guy, so why was a pregnant, 18 year old with a son, his first choice? I don't know.

"What are you doing today?" he asked.

"I'm busy," I replied.

"Damn, a brother can't come chill with you?" he asked chuckling.

"Why do you constantly come for me Marlon? I'm pregnant, and I have an 11-month-old son," I said rubbing my stomach, and frowning because of my aching back.

"That should show you how bad I want you. I don't care about none of that shit," he replied. "Let me take you out this weekend," he added.

"Marlon"

"Pleeeeaaaassseee," he begged like a little kid.

"Okay, okay," I chuckled.

"Aight, I will be at your house to get you around 7pm."

"Okay," I replied and disconnected.

I pulled the manual back out, and looked over it. I looked up at all the pieces of the crib spread everywhere. I had been trying to do this all morning, and was only able to attach one part before needing a snack break. The diaper-changing table was already built, courtesy of Julius thank God. I lay on my back and stared at the ceiling, because I was so damn tired from dragging this big belly around.

"Mrs. Tate, Mr. Tate is here," Winnie said standing in the doorway.

As I sat up as Julius walked into the room. He closed the door behind him, and then joined me on the floor. He rubbed my belly, and then kissed my lips softly. His Dolce and Gabanna cologne smelled so good, and it brought back so many good memories. He was wearing an army green crew neck, dark jeans, and black Roshe Nikes. His peanut butter complexion was looking lickable, and so were his full lips. He lifted his black hat up a bit, to kiss me deeper.

"You can't kiss me."

"Why I can't?" he asked biting his sexy bottom lip.

"Cause we are broken up," I smiled.

. . .

"You my wife, we can't just break up," he said in between kisses.

"What are you doing here?" I asked, pushing him away playfully.

"Winnie called me and said you needed help," he smiled, and I melted. He was so fine, and I wanted him so bad. I needed to be strong though.

"I don't need help," I replied.

"Looks like you do," he said looking around the room.

I ended up sitting there the whole time, watching him build the crib. He was doing a good job on his own, so there was no need for me to get up and help. Winnie brought some Lemon Pepper tuna casserole, which I scarfed down, while watching Julius finish up an hour later.

"Aight, looks good," he said, as he rocked the crib a bit to make sure it was stable.

"Thank you," I replied standing up with my empty plate.

I walked out the room and went to put Jackson in bed for a nap. I wanted him to take a nap since I was taking one. I needed our sleep schedules to be the same. Once he was down, I walked into my bedroom, and Julius was sitting on the bed with his shoes and hat off.

"Get out of here, I'm about to take a nap," I frowned.

"We can take one together," he smiled and tapped the bed.

I rolled my eyes, and walked over to the bed. I took off my maternity pants, and the shirt I was wearing; I always slept like this, I wasn't trying to entice him. He watched me lustfully, as I peeled the comforter back.

"You're the sexiest pregnant woman I've ever seen," he commented.

"Thanks," I replied being short.

I climbed into the bed, and lay on my back. It was the only comfortable position, at this stage of being pregnant. Next thing I knew, I felt Julius' hand caress my belly. It felt good, so I didn't stop him. It was actually helping me fall asleep faster. Being typical Julius, that hand soon went down and tugged on my panties.

"Julius, no," I said pushing his hand.

He got up, pulled off his crew neck and jeans, and then got back into the bed. He slid under the covers of our huge bed, and then positioned his head between my legs. He threw the covers off of us, and pulled my panties off. I couldn't sit up fast enough to stop him, because of my big stomach. He placed my thighs on his shoulders, and licked slowly between the slit.

"Ah," I moaned softly.

He kept licking between the slit, nice and slow, making me get wetter. He placed his big hands on my stomach, and I placed my small ones on top of his, as he sucked on my clit gently. He dipped his tongue in my hole, and then trailed back up to suck on my clit again. I had to grab onto the sheets, as I felt my orgasm rising. I exploded, and he continued making love to my pussy.

"Juuu, I'm tired," I whined.

He ignored me, and kept working his magic on me. I came again, and he licked me clean. He kissed my lower lips a couple times, softly, and then stood on his knees. He pulled his dick out, and I tensed up in anticipation. Whenever we went more than a week without having sex, it hurt. He lowered himself closer to me, and placed the head at my opening.

"Relax baby girl," he whispered.

He pushed one of my legs back a little more, after he couldn't get inside, for more access. He finally got the head in, and then pushed himself in, inch by inch.

"Fuck," he groaned, once all his eleven inches were deep inside me.

"This hurts," I whimpered.

"Just bear with me babe. Ahh," he moaned.

"Oooh. Ju," I cooed as he slowly pumped into me.

The sight of his ab muscles flexing with each thrust, was so sexy. He stared down into my eyes, biting his lip, and then smiled once he felt me cumming.

"Damn I love you Nat," he whispered as he threw his head back.

Tonight I was going to see Natalia again. I was trying to slowly work my way back into her life. I don't know where she thought she was going, but she wasn't going anywhere. I loved her and Jackson more than anything, and Bianca was not about to mess that up for me.

I pulled up to our house, and grabbed the bouquet of roses I'd bought for her. Natalia loved red roses. She was really into romantic movies, so anything like that, always made her smile. I dusted off my black windbreaker, and headed up to the door. I reached into my jean pocket for the key and walked in. I walked through the foyer, and followed the sound of the TV, which led me to the den. I spotted Winnie sitting on the couch watching TV, and Jackson sitting in his playpen.

"Winnie, where is Natalia?" I asked and walked over to pick up Jackson.

"Oh, Mr. Tate, she umm... she" Winnie stammered.

"Where is she Winnie? Is she okay?" I frowned and kissed Jackson's cheek.

"She went to Magnolias Mr. Tate," Winnie half-smiled.

"Magnolia's? With whom? Paula?" I frowned and Winnie shook her head no. The look she was giving me, let me know Natalia was there with somebody she shouldn't have been with.

I put Jackson back in his playpen, and left the roses in the den. I damn near ran out to my car and sped to Magnolias. Really Natalia? She had me fucked up right now. I pulled up after what felt like forever, and parked my shit quickly. I walked in past the hostess, and searched the restaurant frantically for Natalia. I spotted her sitting across from that same nigga I beat up at the club.

"Well, well, well," I said walking up to their table.

"Julius..." Natalia said with her eyes bucked. Her long brown hair was down, and she had on a short black dress.

"Oh my goodness," the dude exhaled, wiping a hand over his face.

"What the fuck you doing here with this nigga?" I frowned.

"We aren't together Julius, you can't do this," she said in a low tone.

I sat down next to her, and dipped my tongue in her mouth. She tried to pull away, but I wasn't allowing that shit. I sucked on her lips and rubbed her belly, as her little date commented and groaned. Natalia finally pushed me away after a nice tongue down.

"Really Natalia? This what you want?" I asked pointing to her little date.

"Leave Julius, please," she replied.

"Aight, remember this ma," I said as I hopped up and bounced. My phone buzzed in my pocket on the way out, and it was Franceska.

Franceska: So how long you gone ignore me daddy?

Me: Where are you?

Franceska: My new condo, I moved here.

Wow, this dick I'm working with must be a game changer, if all these bitches is relocating for it.

Me: Oh.

Franceska: Come over.

Me: Send your address.

As I waited for her address, a text from Natalia came through.

Wife: Don't go messing with other girls.

Me: Oh but you can go on dates? Get the fuck outta here.

Wife: I'm not on a date. I'm out with a friend. Plus, we are broken up.

Me: So if we broke up, then it shouldn't matter who I'm messing with.
Wife: It does.
Me: Why?
Wife: Cause I need to see that you have discipline!
Me: Whatever, have fun on your date. If you let that nigga hit, I'm killing both of y'all.
Wife: I love you too much to do that. Now you prove that you feel the same.

Damn, now I was wondering if I should even go see Franceska. Why shouldn't I though? She up in here with this nigga, and then gone diss me in front of him. She lucky I didn't bust that nigga in his face, in front of all those people, telling me to leave and shit. Nah fuck that, I been showing her how much I love her. One little quick fuck ain't gone hurt.

"Took you long enough," Franceska smacked her lips as she opened her door. She walked away from the door, and her fat ass was jiggling around her red thong. Her house was dark, and the only light was coming from the TV.

"Whatever," I said closing and locking it.

I was feeling bad as hell for being here, and I didn't like it. I couldn't get hard, when all I had was Natalia's feelings on my mind. I needed to drink or smoke, so I could do this shit. *Just leave Julius. Nope fuck that.* My mind kept switching back and forth.

"Want some?" Franceska asked, as she lifted some Gin.

"Yeah," I nodded.

She flashed me her pretty smile and threw her long, curly weave behind her shoulders. She poured my drink, and then handed it to me as she took a pull on her blunt.

"So what made you finally answer my texts?" she asked blowing out smoke.

"Don't worry about all that. Just be glad I answered," I chuckled and so did she.

She put her blunt out, and then straddled me in her skimpy attire. I tipped my glass up and finished the gin that was left in it. I rubbed up her small back, then back down to cuff her fat ass.

"I missed you so much Ju," she purred in her little Spanish accent, as she kissed my neck.

Stop thinking about your wife Julius, I thought. I held onto Franceska, and then reached to pour myself another glass with my free hand. I downed the Gin, and then immediately unhooked Franceska's bra. Her tattoo of my name was now in clear view.

"I'm so in love with you Ju," she moaned as I licked her hard nipples. I just wanna be with you baby," she added as she ground her hips on my pelvis. Would she shut the fuck up? Damn!

I pulled my shirt and windbreaker off, and she started to plant kisses on my chest. Her lips were soft as fuck, and I smiled 'cause I was getting in the mood finally. I quickly pulled my dick out, and ripped the condom package open with my teeth. I rolled it down, and ripped her thin panties off. I turned her around, and slid her down onto my dick. I watched her ass bounce, as she went up down.

"Fuck, I'm about to cum Ju. I love you so fucking much," she cried out and then gushed on my pole.

"Mmm, fuck," I said under my breath damn near.

She turned around, and slid back down on to my dick. I took her nipple into my mouth, as she bounced up and down on me. This shit was feeling like heaven, but I'd much rather be inside my wife. I lifted her legs over my arms, and she leaned back to speed up her pace.

"Ahhh, fuck daddy," she yelled as she scrunched up her face.

Soon enough, we exploded together, and guilt consumed me. This was probably one of the worst nuts I've ever busted in my twenty-one years. I knew Natalia was gone fuck my head up when I first met her ass, and I was right.

I moved Franceska off me, went to flush the condom, and then got dressed. I don't even remember if I said bye or not before I left. I sped to the house I shared with Natalia, hoping she was home by now. It was 11pm; she'd better be fucking home.

I walked into the house, and all the lights were out. I headed to the bathroom to take a shower before seeing Natalia. I didn't want to use the bathroom in our room, because she may get suspicious. After I got out, I went into our bedroom, and threw on some boxers and joggers, before hopping in the bed with my wife. I cuddled up behind her, and kissed the tattoo of our wedding date on the nape of her neck. She stirred a bit, and then placed her small hands over mine, which were on her protruding belly.

"I love you Nat," I whispered.

"I love you too Ju," she replied in a whisper as well.

We needed to stop playing these fucking games and just be back together.

BIANCA

All that shit Julius was spitting to me about being faithful to Natalia was bullshit. I sat outside for an hour, while he fucked some random bitch. I stayed out there even after he left, because I wanted to know who the fuck she was.

What pisses me off, is the fact that he was yapping about his love for his wife, but making time for this hoe. That just showed me that all the stuff he was saying to me was a bunch of bullshit. He could never be over me that quickly, Julius loved me whether he wanted to believe it or not.

Since he hadn't been answering my damn calls, I planned to show up to his little club and talk to his ass. I needed to confront him about this little Spanish bitch he decided to have on the side. Maybe I could blackmail him into fucking with me. I don't know, but I will think of something.

"What you need?" some nigga answered the club door. It was around 1pm so it wasn't open yet.

"I need to speak to Julius," I spat.

"He expecting you?" he asked with an attitude.

"Yes, it's about our son," I said rubbing my fake belly.

"Oh, I need to check with him"

"Nigga move!" I shouted slipping by him.

He grabbed my arm, but I snatched away from him. I stormed to the back and headed up the stairs to his office. I saw the wooden door, and it was slightly cracked open. I knocked lightly, and then just walked in.

"Henry!" Julius called out.

"Sup bro? I tried to stop her," Henry said peeking in.

"It's that easy to get by you? I will deal with you in a second," Julius said shaking his head. "Fuck you doing here B?" Julius asked once Henry left.

"I'm just a little taken aback," I replied sitting down. "I saw you cheating on your wife two nights ago," I smiled.

"Okay, you can leave," he said shaking his head. I saw his eyes were low under his cap, showing he was high. He had on a red polo, and his wrist was iced out. His cologne filled the air every time he moved, and he was sucking on his favorite jolly rancher. Damn, I loved me some Julius Tate.

"Look Julius, don't make me send the pictures I took to your little wife. All you have to do is give me some of your time," I said folding my arms over my chest.

"Are you actually coming in here and threatening me? Do you hear how thirsty and pathetic you sound Bianca? You trying to blackmail a nigga to be with you," he chuckled. "Wow, you've hit rock bottom ma," he said shaking his head.

I did feel pathetic, but at this point I didn't care. I had come too far to care about how I looked. Nothing was worse than lying about a pregnancy, so I could care less.

"Call it what you want. Now do we have a deal?' I raised a brow.

"Nah, we don't. So if you want to send some pictures, go right ahead. Natalia and I aren't even together right now," he said, still chuckling at my expense.

"Julius, stop doing this to me!" I yelled frustrated. I had no picture evidence. I assumed he would cave, and beg me not to send these non-existent pictures.

"Aight, get the fuck up," he said lifting me up off of the couch.

"Get off me," I screamed, squirming like a crazy person, as Julius damn near dragged me out his place.

"I don't want to hear from you until the baby gets here, so we can test him," he said after throwing me out the door.

"I hate you!" I yelled loud as hell, as the club door shut.

People were walking by, looking at me like I was crazy. I was starting to look at myself the same way. I was starting to feel less, and less sane by the minute.

Marlon and I had been somewhat dating on the low for a couple weeks now. I didn't know what the hell I was doing. Julius would still spend the night sometimes, but we wouldn't have sex. We would only go to sleep together, and after he bathed Jackson in the morning, he would leave.

This evening, I was going over Marlon's house, because he was going to cook for me. I know I shouldn't allow him to do all this when I still want to be with Julius, but maybe my mind would change. Maybe after spending some time with him, I would want to be with him. Then again, I can't ever see myself getting Julius out of my system.

I wasn't gonna get dressed up at all, because I felt I was too big to do that. I put on a black tube dress that stopped mid-thigh, and some black sandals. I put my chestnut brown hair in a ponytail, and then headed out. I passed up a mirror in the hallway, and stared at my chain that Julius had given me. He hadn't hit me in forever, and I hadn't heard about him sleeping around. I smiled in the mirror at my thoughts, before heading to Jackson's room. He was asleep, so I kissed his cheek and then said bye to Winnie as I headed out the door.

"You took a while, but it was worth the wait," Marlon smiled.

"Thank you," I replied.

"Anytime," he replied looking me up and down. How was he even attracted to me with this big belly? "Well come in ma," he chuckled and moved out the doorway.

I walked into his apartment, and it seemed so small compared to my home with Julius. I nodded in approval, hoping he didn't know what I was really thinking. His place reminded me of where I lived with my mother back in Indianapolis. It wasn't bad at all, but it was nothing to brag about.

"Would you like some cranberry apple cider?" Marlon asked as I sat on the couch.

"Yes please," I smiled.

He walked away, and I heard the oven open in the kitchen. It made me wonder if Julius could cook. I was the one always cooking for him; Winnie or me. I loved cooking for him though, because he always acted like I was the greatest chef ever.

"Why you smiling?" Marlon asked, returning with my cider. *Stop thinking about your husband Natalia!* I thought.

"I'm just thinking about how nice this is," I lied and smiled.

"I see," Marlon nodded, and sat next to me with a beer. "Can I ask you something Natalia?" he finally spoke after about a minute of silence.

"Okay," I responded.

"What's up with you and that husband of yours?" he frowned.

"We are separated," I replied.

"Y'all have a legal separation?" he raised a brow. *Legal separation? What the hell is that?*

"Yeah," I lied not even knowing what it was.

"So what was all that shit the other day, when we were on a date?" he quizzed.

"Oh, h-he's just having a hard time letting go."

"Is he the only one having a hard time?" he asked suspiciously.

"Yeah… why?" I frowned.

"Because I sat there and witnessed you guys kissing for a nice minute, before you finally pushed him off you."

"Oh. Marlon, I'm hungry," I said trying to change the subject.

"Natalia, I need answers," he said sternly.

"Okay, goodnight. I'm eight months pregnant, and I need food, not twenty-one questions," I said standing up slowly.

"Wait, wait. Chill. Let's go eat," he smiled helping me up. I smiled back at him and headed to the kitchen.

For the rest of the night, we had pretty good conversation, but it was hard to get Julius out of my head. Marlon tried to kiss me, but I told him it was too much too soon. As soon as I got home, I smelled Julius' Dolce and Gabanna cologne in the foyer. I walked to, and up the stairs, before entering the bedroom. All the lights were off, but the moon shined just enough through our window, for me to see. Julius was lying in bed, looking on his phone.

"Where you been? You was with him?" he asked and looked up from his phone. The backlight of it was shining on his abs.

"Ye-yeah," I said as I neared the bed. I pulled my tube dress over my head, and dropped it into the chair.

Julius locked his phone, and then put it on the nightstand. He pulled my side of the covers back, and I climbed in. He cuddled up behind me, wrapped his arms around my body, and then palmed my belly.

"At least you know who to come home to," he whispered and kissed the corner of my mouth.

I didn't respond, and we both soon drifted off to sleep.

"Thank you for giving me a ride Julius," Franceska smiled as we walked towards the doctor's office.

I wouldn't have even gotten out, but it was too hot outside. She said she was gonna be quick, so I didn't want to go somewhere just to have to come right back. I was only doing this shit, because out of all the bitches I fucked with besides Natalia, Franceska had never fucked me over. Fuck. Speaking of Natalia, she was walking out of the doctor building with Lucy.

"Really?" she frowned up at me.

"Baby, I'm just giving her a"

"A what Julius? The same thing you was giving her in that hotel room?" Natalia yelled, and tears started to well up in her eyes.

"Come on babe," Franceska had the nerve to say.

"Babe?" Natalia bucked her eyes. "Bitch, you lucky I'm pregnant," she glared at her.

"Natalia, relax baby girl," I said grabbing her arm.

"Don't touch me," she spat calmly and snatched her arm. "I want a divorce," she added.

"Well too damn bad! We ain't doing nothing Natalia! I'm doing her a favor by taking her to the doctor!"

"Oh, is she having your baby too? How many you about to have now, Ju?" Natalia frowned.

"She is not having my baby! You are the only one having my baby right now. Not her, nor Bianca," I shrugged.

"Come on Lucy," Natalia said walking off.

"Natalia... Natalia!" I called after her and she didn't turn around. "Don't you ever in yo' fucking life, address me as nothing other than Julius in front of my wife. You got that?" I said through gritted teeth to Franceska. My face was so close to hers that I could feel the air coming out of her nose.

"I'm sorry Ju, I"

"You did know. Get another fucking ride home," I spat, and walked off to my car, ignoring Franceska like Natalia had done me.

Once I got to the parking lot, I saw Natalia was still there. I jogged over, and lightly grabbed her arm.

"Nat, I swear to God babe. This was an innocent friendly gesture," I said with my hands in prayer mode.

"Why are you friends with a girl that you cheated on me with?" she frowned up at me.

"So now I can't have friends?" I frowned back.

"No! Not ones that you have had sex with Julius! You cheated on me with her! Do you love her or something?!" she cried.

"No babe. Hell no! I was just being nice. But if I can't have friends, then you can't be hanging out with ole boy," I said.

"What? He and I are just friends. He's never stuck his dick inside me."

"And he better not ever. Nor put his lips on any part of you. He better not even know what you look like without clothes," I glared down at her.

"Bye Ju," she said shaking her head, and walking back to the car.

"I love you Mrs. Tate!" I yelled after her and she flicked me off.

I was relaxing on the couch, thinking about how I ran into Julius earlier. It seemed like he would never change. I hated him so much, yet loved him so much. He and Jackson were my everything, but I couldn't let him walk all over my heart anymore.

I looked over at my son sleeping on his tummy, and turned down the TV so it wouldn't wake him. My phone buzzed, just as I was turning on Netflix. I looked over and saw it was Marlon calling.

"Hello?"

"How you feeling?" he asked.

"I'm okay. You?"

"I'm doing okay, I would be better if I could see you," he said, sounding like he was smiling.

"You really want to be with me?"

"Hell yeah Natalia, can't you see that by now baby?"

"Okay boyfriend," I chuckled.

"For real?" he asked sounding excited.

"Unless you"

"No! Hell no! I mean yes, girlfriend," he laughed. "Can I come see you tonight?" he asked.

"No, I'm relaxing right now. But we can go somewhere tomorrow," I offered.

"Cool, see you tomorrow babe."

"Goodnight," I replied and hung up. What was I doing? They say the easiest way to get over someone, is by getting someone else, so I was gonna try it.

I smiled and lay back on my pillow, when suddenly my water broke.

"Winnie!" I called out as I clutched my stomach.

"Yes Mrs. Tate?" she came running in.

"My water broke. I need you to take me to the hospital, and call Julius!" I screamed.

JULIUS

ONE HOUR EARLIER

Bianca had the baby, and she called me over to come see him. She said I needed to hurry up because he was gonna be sleep soon. I didn't care if he was sleep, but I was interested to see if he looked like me. I was a little upset that she didn't tell me she was giving birth, since I had been unblocked her in my phone. She just randomly hit me up thirty minutes ago, and said to meet her at her apartment.

Before stopping by, I went to CVS and grabbed one of those DNA tests. She tried to play me by not having it done at the hospital, but that shit wasn't gone work. I needed this test done, because I was anxious to know. I would still get another one from a professional, just to double check in case she tried to discredit this one.

"About time," Bianca said, as her eyes searched behind me frantically.

"You good?" I asked as I walked in.

"Yeah, come on!" she said closing and locking her front door, and then walking to the back.

I followed her to her bedroom, and the baby was laying on Bianca's bed sleep. I smiled 'cause he looked nothing like me, but then again, I needed to know for sure. Looks only meant so much. She said he was a premature baby but he looked regular sized to me.

"What the hell are you doing nigga?" Bianca frowned as she saw me opening the kit.

"I'm about to test this little nigga," I replied, confused as to why she was surprised.

"No you're not!" she yelled lunging towards me.

I moved swiftly out the way, and she hit her dresser. She stood up and charged me again. We fell back on her bed, as she tried to wrestle the kit out my hand.

"Bianca, get the fuck up! You gone hurt the baby!" I yelled pushing her.

Just as she hit the floor, I heard her front door bust open. I hopped off the bed, and headed out the bedroom, only to run dead smack into a couple police officers. One walked past me, and picked Bianca up off the floor. He started to handcuff her, and the other started to handcuff me.

"Wait, what the fuck is going on here?" I asked squirming.

"You all are under arrest for child abduction," the officer cuffing me replied.

BECOME A VIP READER!

*To join my mailing list text **SHVONNE** to **66866** and stay up to date! Also, join **Shvonne Latrice Reading Group** on Facebook!*